# THE NEXT FILES
## DOUBLE PUZZLER


# BUNYIP

And

# HELLHOUSE


by

G L Keady

Published in Australia in 2024
by Big Island Publishing



**Big Island Publishing**
PO Box 3027, Tuross Head, 2537, NSW, Australia
www.bigislandpublishing.au

ISBN:
E-book: 9780975633083
Print: 9780975633090

Edited by: Canon Doyle
Cover design: Brandon Evans-Keady

# TABLE OF CONTENTS


Chapter One ...........................................................7

Chapter Two ......................................................... 12

Chapter Three ....................................................... 18

Chapter Four ........................................................23

Chapter Five .........................................................28

Chapter Six...........................................................33

Chapter Seven .......................................................38

Chapter Eight .......................................................44

Chapter Nine ........................................................49

Chapter Ten ..........................................................54

Chapter Eleven......................................................59


**HELLHOUSE**


Chapter One ...........................................................69

Chapter Two .........................................................75

Chapter Three........................................................80

Chapter Four ........................................................86

Chapter Five .........................................................91

Chapter Six...........................................................97

Chapter Seven ...................................................... 102

Chapter Eight ...................................................... 108

# CHAPTER ONE

Wearing earbuds that played 'Girl of the World', one of her favourite tracks, Mirren Butler tussled with the unsteady old gate of Mont House. It's an abandoned, rundown farmhouse sitting on Yanco Creek. The moon was full and yellow overhead, casting an eerie shadow over the house from a big, dead blue gum at the driveway's side.

Mirren is a Wiradjuri girl, working as a junior heritage officer for Parks, Heritage and Wildlife. She oversees six heritage estates, including Mont House. She drove her Rav 4 through the gate and pulled up at the homestead. Fresh from graduating Leeton High and new on the job, she had P plates on the council car. Mont House was her last stop on her weekly rounds, and she was late, not planning on checking for vandalism in the dark.

She left the headlights on, took out her earbuds, grabbed her torch, and stepped out of the car, heading for the porch steps. The single-storey weatherboard house had a menacing look, with windows on either side of the front door like eyes and a weird curved door arch resembling an angry mouth. The wind was picking up, hinting at the spring storm on the way, with lightning flashing in the south.

The floorboards creaked under Mirren's work boots. A gust of wind brought a strange sound—a mix of a dog's howl and a croaky growl, something she'd never heard before. She ignored it, scanning the area with her torch, confirming everything was secure. She checked the CCTV on the eave, its red light blinking, showing it was sending digital images back to the office via satellite. Job done, she waved at the CCTV, then turned to leave.

 

But then, a loud, unearthly scream stopped her dead. She swung her torch towards the creek, where the noise had come from. Suddenly feeling very alone in the dark, she bravely, tentatively, started towards the tree line edging the swampy creek, about 100 metres away.

The wind intensified, sending her long black hair streaming out like a banner; the storm was drawing closer—thunder rolled in the distance. A sudden crack resounded, and her torchlight revealed a Weeping Willow, where the large, intense eyes of an owl stared back at her. Winding through the trees, Mirren reached a stagnant billabong, a relic of the last flood, with the murmuring of Yanco Creek audible in the distance. Suddenly, the harmonious nocturnal chorus of frogs and crickets fell silent, leaving the world around her eerily quiet. She stood still, a chill running down her spine. The tales from her elders echoed in her mind, warning of supernatural occurrences heralded by such silence. A loud splash from the billabong made her spin around, her torch illuminating a floating cow, its body gruesomely ripped open... truly gross. The reeds along the billabong's bank rustled violently ... something was moving through them, something low and swift. As she cast the light through the reeds, trying to spot the source, she caught a fleeting glimpse of something otherworldly, unlike anything she had ever seen or imagined. In that heart-stopping moment, Mirren knew, deep down, it had to be a bunyip.

With his cowboy boots propped up on the desk, his father's hat tipped back on his head, and blowing big purple bubblegum bubbles, Digger was utterly engrossed in the email he'd just received.

"Hey!" Jax exclaimed, entering abruptly, startling Digger nearly out of his skin.

"Jax, you scared the heck out of me!"

Jax sauntered over, "Oh sorry, didn't mean to ... What's got you so jumpy?"

"This email from a Wiradjuri girl. She had a close encounter with a bunyip."

"Seriously? I thought bunyips were just in Aboriginal folklore, you know, lurking in billabongs and riverbeds, waiting to snatch livestock, women, and kids … that kind of stuff."

"Yeah, that's what I always thought. But wait till you read this … She's legit, works for Parks and Wildlife."

Jax's interest piqued. "Where exactly?"

"Leeton."

"Should've guessed when you mentioned Wiradjuri. Their country includes Narrandera, Yanco, Leeton… Wiradjuri means 'running water', right? After the Murrumbidgee River."

"Yeah, 'Murrumbidgee' translates to 'big water' in Wiradjuri. Here, take a look…" He swivelled his monitor for her to read the email. After a quick scan, Jax said, "So she wants us to check it out?"

"Yep. Locals think it's typical cattle mutilation," Digger explained.

"Like from aliens?"

"That's one guess … The newspaper in Wagga Wagga reported it but didn't specify. No mention of a bunyip or aliens. They hinted at dingoes."

"Dingoes wouldn't do that to a cow," Jax stated matter-of-factly.

"It would make a cracking 'Next Files' story," Digger chuckled, eager for a trip out of town.

"You just want to hit the bush," Jax observed, raising an eyebrow knowingly.

"Think you can persuade Doc?"

"Probably. He loves debunking myths. He'd jump at the chance."

An hour later, Jax was in Carter's office, laying out the story for him. Carter, in his typical pitch-receiving mode, sat behind his desk, rotating a pen between his fingers while slightly swaying in his big office chair. After Jax finished her pitch, a pause filled the room. Carter halted his swivelling and pen-twirling, clearly having reached a decision.

"Hmm, the bunyip falls into the same category as the yowie, Australia's version of sasquatch, the yeti and bigfoot … I'm not sure if a cattle mutilation will thrill our city audience."

"That wouldn't be my angle boss, like it's about the horror this teenage Wiradjuri girl, Mirren Butler experienced at this old abandoned Mont House. Digger's idea is for us stay a few nights there and film it, hand held…"

"I get it like the Blair Witch Project?"

"Yep, something like that."

"Well if it gets the audience it got in 1999, but it was a mockumentary, is that your intention?"

"No. I won't risk losing the integrity of The Next Files."

"Good to hear," he said, resuming his pen-twiddling. "Run it past Janet, if you get her approval it's a go."

"Thanks boss."

As she was getting up to leave, Carter asked, "By the way when's Tilly back?"

"According to Digger the next day or two."

"And Doc, haven't seen him around?"

"After Janet, I'll need to pitch bunyip to him."

"Good luck with that," he said with a sceptical glint in his eye.

Jax entered the Friend in Hand pub, expecting to find Doc playing his usual game of darts. True to form, there he was, sitting with a couple of mates, enjoying a beer. Doc looked up as she approached and said cynically, "Ah, if it isn't queen Jax." His comment drew a raucous laugh from his three companions.

Blushing and a bit embarrassed, Jax folded her arms and rolled her eyes. "Done?"

Doc grinned. "Ease up, Jax. I was just telling these guys about our last crazy adventure."

Jax wasn't in the mood for small talk. "Need to talk to you, in private."

Doc got up, "Sure thing, let's hit the bar. Looks like you need a drink."

As they made their way to the bar, Doc shared a light-hearted story. "My mate Bevan was just telling us he was visiting his sister yesterday when he came out of her place, the house across the street was being auctioned. He saw a friend of his in the auction, gave him a wave and bought the house."

Jax cracked a smile. "For real? Or you just messing with me?"

"Nope, just trying to get a smile out of you. So, what's up?"

They sat on stools at the bar. Doc ordered a couple of beers, and Jax filled him in on the bunyip story. Waiting for his reaction, she watched as he mulled it over. Finally, he said, "The cattle mutilation angle is interesting. I've read about instances in the States, blaming it on aliens doing experiments or something. Doesn't make a lot of sense that an alien species would travel the galaxy to visit an outback town to autopsy a cow."

"I agree, which is why Digger and I favour the bunyip scenario."

"Isn't that just Aboriginal myth?"

"Yes, but there have been sightings of it since colonisation."

"What's it look like?"

Jax handed over her phone, and as he looked at depictions of the bunyip, he read aloud, "'Descriptions vary enormously, from feathered alligators to large seal-like monsters and even giant three-horned toads. Some have suggested that the mythology may have originated from the early Aboriginal people's encounters with megafauna, the giant marsupials that occupied the continent thousands of years ago. The bunyip was believed by the Aboriginals to have supernatural powers'… now that doesn't surprise me… This is interesting, 'In 1857 an Edwin Stocqueler travelled on the Murray and Goulburn rivers, where six times he sighted a large freshwater seal, having two small paddles or fins attached to the shoulders, a long swan like neck, a head like a dog, and a curious bag hanging under the jaw, resembling the pouch of the pelican. The animal was covered with hair, like the platypus, and the colour a glossy black. This he claimed was a bunyip.'"

"So, what do you think? Are you onboard to debunk a myth?"

# CHAPTER
# TWO

Later, at Tilly's house, they were all gathered around a table in the sunroom. Jax, Digger, and Doc were deep in planning mode for their trip to Mont House. Digger, fidgeting with a digital camera, complained, "Don't know why I have to be the cameraman."

"It's your idea for the Blair Witch-style shoot," Jax reminded him.

"I'm not so great with gadgets," Digger grumbled.

Doc, with a somewhat dour expression, offered, "Give it here then … If I could handle the camera on our last trip, I can manage this one too."

Digger handed over the Sony camcorder with relief. "Yeah, well, just keep it dry, okay?"

Jax joked, "I don't think we'll be doing any white water rafting on this one."

"So, you want it all Blair Witch-like, hand-held, reality TV style?" Doc clarified.

"That's what Janet wants," Jax said. "She thinks the less editing, the more convincing it'll be."

"Won't be convincing if nothing happens," Doc pointed out.

Digger, with a hint of mystery, said, "I don't know … I've got a weird feeling about this one."

Digger and Jax exchanged a solemn look, which Doc, busy inspecting the camera, missed. "So, what's the game plan?"

"I've talked to Mirren," Jax replied. "She's sorted out Mont House for us and will stay the three days. We just need enough supplies to last."

"Is there anything at the house, like power, running water, eating utensils?" asked Doc.

"There's power, but it's a heritage site, pretty much unchanged since 1907. So, no electric lights, just candles, and no power outlets. It's got a wood stove, but we'll need to bring our own cutlery and stuff. Oh, and no fridge or beds."

"So, not exactly an AirBNB, huh?" Doc quipped with a smile.

"Nope, it's pretty basic. Think sleeping bags and rations."

"Will we be armed?" inquired Digger.

"Mirren will be," Jax replied.

"Okay, I'll ask the obvious question, what happened in 1907 for it to be vacated until now?"

"In that year three Wiradjuri, a man, his woman and their 4-year-old boy, were making their way along Yanco Creek looking for tucker, it was getting near dark, so they set up camp next to billabong, only a hundred metres from the Mont homestead. During the night it is believe a creature emerged from the swampy waters of the billabong, attacked the campsite and ate the little boy. The man managed to spear the monster but it had no effect, it came after them. They ran to the Mont homestead for help. Living there was Alister Mont and his wife Victoria. Banging on the door and screaming woke them. It was 3 am, Mont grabbed his rifle and answered the door. "Okay, I'll ask the obvious question, what happened in 1892 for it to be vacated until now?" Doc queried.

"Well, in that year, three Wiradjuri people—a man, his partner, and their 4-year-old kid—were traveling along Yanco Creek, hunting for tucker. It was getting dark, so they camped near a billabong, just a hundred metres from the Mont homestead. During the night, it is believed a creature came out of the swampy waters of the billabong, attacked their camp, and took the little boy. The man tried to spear the creature, but it didn't stop; it came after them. They ran to Mont House for help. Alister Mont and his wife Victoria lived there. The banging and screaming woke them up around 3 am. Mont grabbed his rifle and went to answer the door." When he opened it, he found the two Wiradjuri on the porch, torn to pieces, and no sign of what had attacked them, just this weird guttural sound, like a large crocodile, coming from the darkness.

Victoria was so freaked out by it, they sold up and left. Rumours spread, and the place has been deserted ever since."

"So, Mont didn't actually see anything?" Doc asked.

"No, the police combed the area the next day, including the billabong, and came up empty, except a black tracker found a set of huge, webbed footprints leading from the billabong to the house and back to the water. There wasn't a proper autopsy, but a Leeton doctor examined the bodies and reckoned they'd been mauled by a large creature with claws. He'd seen similar wounds from a croc attack in Queensland. No crocs have ever been reported that far south in New South Wales, but in saying that, 2019, a skinned croc was found on the bank of the Murray River near Mildura. The Murrumbidgee, where Yanco Creek is a tributary, meets the Murray there."

"Yeah," Digger chimed in, "And the whole river system is fed by the Barka, right from near Queensland, so a croc might have made it down to Yanco."

"The Barka? Never heard of that," Doc said, puzzled.

"It's the Darling River. The Koori call it the Barka," Jax clarified.

"So, it could've been a massive croc?" Doc pondered.

"I doubt it," Digger countered, "But if there's been a croc or anything strange, the local Wiradjuri would likely know. Stuff like that usually shows up in their art."

"That seems like a solid place to start," Doc agreed. "When do we head out? I've got a gig tonight."

"Oh cool, where?" Digger asked.

"The Friend in Hand. Come along, bring your harp and didge and jam with us."

Digger's face lit up with excitement. Jax, seeing his eagerness, said, "Sure, we'll come. But I want to head to Leeton by midday tomorrow."

Seated at the bar of the Friend in Hand, Jax had a great view across the crowded room to the stage. She sipped her beer and watched with pride as Digger joined in with backup vocals, complementing Doc's lead performance of 'Falling.' The vibe in the pub was buzzing, and the music added to the lively atmosphere, offering a moment of relaxation and enjoyment before their upcoming adventure to Mont House.

Well, there's twenty thousand faces
All standing in a line
Each one wants to get the job
But only one will sign
We're falling, falling, free falling.

There's trouble in the city
That's what the papers say
But you can't believe
In all you read
It's a game we told to play
We're falling, falling, free falling

And all I want is my freedom
All I ask is my right
All I want is my freedom
That's the right to life my kind of life.

Yeah!
All right…

We pay our rates and taxes
They bleed our pockets dry
And when we haven't got
A penny left
It's tears of blood they cry
We're falling, falling, free falling

We have to slave and suffer
Until we're sixty-five
To work our way
Into the grave
Then even pay to die
We're falling, falling, free falling

And all I want is my freedom
All I ask is my right
All I want is my freedom
And the right to life my kind of life.

Doc ripped into a powerful guitar solo, then seamlessly transitioned back into the vocals.

We're falling, falling, free falling...
And all I want is my freedom
All I ask is my right
All I want is my freedom
That's the right to life my kind of life.

All I want is my freedom
All I ask is my right
All I want is my freedom
And the right to life my kind of life.

All I want is my freedom
And all I ask is my right
All I want is my freedom
And the right to life my kind of life.

The crowd was totally hyped as Doc nailed the solo outro. The buzz and energy were awesome, filling up the whole room. Jax found herself standing and clapping along with everyone else, shouting for an encore.

The next day at 1:25 PM, the Regional Express Saab 340 landed at Narrandera Airport. Waiting for them was Mirren. Jax and Doc could tell Digger was pretty taken with her right away, and who could blame him? Mirren was not only super pretty but also really easy-going.

The drive to Narrandera was super quick, like six minutes quick, so they didn't get much chance to talk shop. Instead, they just chatted and got to know each other a bit.

Once they got to the Parks and Wildlife office, they were shown to the boardroom and got some cool refreshments and snacks. Mirren then filled them in about her bunyip encounter and shared some stuff about the bunyip legends and science in the area, which was very interesting.

Digger was totally smitten with Mirren, and Jax was sure it was love at first sight. The best part? It looked like Mirren felt the same way.

After they'd all shared what they knew about the bunyip stuff, it was time to hit the road for the forty-minute drive to Mont House.

# CHAPTER
# THREE

As they arrived at the gate to Mont House, the sun was just setting. True to country manners, Digger jumped out to open the gate, letting Mirren drive through. The driveway led them up to the house. At this time of day, the old, ramshackle weatherboard house looked pretty eerie, especially with the massive dead blue gum looming over it like a giant, gnarled beast.

They all stepped out of the car, taking in the scene. The sky was split between an orange streak in the west and inky darkness in the east. A hundred metres away was a thicket of she-oaks and willow trees, and the house in front of them had clearly seen better days.

Mirren led the way onto the porch, gave a casual wave to the CCTV, and unlocked the front door. Doc captured everything on the camcorder, adding his own commentary. The rest of them acted like the camera wasn't even there, treating it and Doc interchangeably, directing any comments they had to the camera as if speaking to Doc himself.

After soaking up the fresh country air, Digger was the last to head into the house. "The trees over there, that's by the billabong, yeah?" he asked Mirren.

"Yeah, that's right. Yanco Creek's just about twenty metres past it," she replied."

"I could hear the creek," Digger said.

"Wow, you've got good hearing," Mirren remarked with a smile. She then headed back to the Rav 4, followed by Digger, to bring in the bags. Meanwhile, Doc filmed Jax doing a tour of inspection.

"Isn't it a bit dark to film?"

"This little beauty has a really cool low-light feature. Hey, listen, how about getting Janet to use some Time Benders' music in the show?"

"That's a great idea."

Jax led Doc towards the kitchen, fighting through a big cobweb across the doorway. She complained, brushing herself down frantically, "Ew! I hate spiders." Stopping in the middle of the kitchen, the flickering light from a lamp carried by Mirren suddenly filled the room. It revealed a lot of dust and not much else.

"There's an old wood oven that we can't use. As a matter of fact, we can't use anything in the house. It's all heritage. So, we'll have to stick to the living room to bunker down," Mirren explained.

"Lucky it's not winter," Jax said.

"You bet, it can get pretty cold here at night," Mirren said, leading them back to the living room. "Anyone hungry?" she asked.

They all shook their heads. Digger said, "I'm pretty keen to check out the billabong. That's where the bunyip's supposed to be from, right?"

Mirren explained, "If it's a real creature, I doubt it's still there. The billabong dries up a lot, especially in droughts. My dad checked it out back in the last drought when it was totally dry and found nothing."

Digger nodded thoughtfully. "Well, I'm sure the Wiradjuri mob might think of it differently."

"Thinking it's something supernatural?" Doc chimed in.

"Speaking of the Wiradjuri," Jax was reminded, "I'd like to speak with elders tomorrow."

"I'm Wiradjuri. We can't visit my great-grandmother; she recently turned a hundred."

"That'd be great, is she cognisant?"

"She's a walking history book of country and its people ... oh, yes, she's cognisant all right, just you wait and see."

Jax was delighted to have such a valuable resource.

Digger called out to Doc, "You coming to the billabong, cameraman?"

Doc shot him a huge grin. "Wouldn't miss it for the world, mate."

"Here, take this Digger," Jax said, handing him a torch.

Digger led the way, with Doc following close behind, filming. Outside, it was mostly dark, with scudding clouds occasionally parting to reveal a waning gibbous moon. The eerie moonlight added a haunting ambiance. If it weren't for the thought of a supernatural monster, it would have been an enjoyable stroll in the countryside. However, the legend of the bunyip cast a threatening shadow over nature. Every slight sound was analysed, every movement scrutinised; they were decidedly on edge. Doc, choosing not to do a running commentary, preferred to capture the natural ambience.

As they reached the trees lining the billabong, the clouds parted, bathing the mirrored surface of the large waterhole in light.

Digger stopped at the bank, turned to the camera, and said, "All looks calm and serene to me. Wiradjuri legend has it that bunyips inhabit billabongs like this one. In fact, a bunyip was blamed for the deaths of a family of three Wiradjuri at this very billabong back in 1907. Now, I don't expect a creature described as a man-eating platypus the size of a cow to still be inhabiting this waterhole. But Wiradjuri legend suggests the bunyip is not a physical monster, but a spiritual one … in other parts of Australia…" His words were abruptly cut off by a loud splash. He turned sharply towards the waterhole, the ripples radiating in rings from the centre, glistening in the moonlight. Shining the torch on the water, then holding it under his chin, eerily lighting his alarmed face, he turned back to the camera, "Um, either a branch or something just fell into the billabong, or something in it swirled… I think we should be getting back to the homestead; we'll investigate in daylight," Digger said nervously. "Cut!" Shining the torch ahead, they rushed back to the house as if something was chasing them.

Jax and Mirren appeared anxious as Doc and Digger recounted their eerie venture to the waterhole and the mysterious loud splash in the water.

"And you know, another weird thing, just before that happened, everything fell deathly quiet," Digger said in a creepy voice. "No crickets, no frogs, no breeze in the trees... nothing. Tell me, Mirren, how deep is the billabong?"

"We think it's about 5 metres, but it changes seasonally. You know, there is something a little odd now that you mention it. I remember Dad telling me after he'd surveyed it when it was empty during the drought... it's fed by an artesian spring at its centre. It wasn't flowing when Dad found it, but he did climb into the cave in the substructure it springs from and discovered quite a large cave system down there."

"If we were to do a magnetometer survey, we could map it," Doc suggested.

"What if it connects with Yanco Creek?" Digger proposed, wide-eyed. The implication that crocodiles could during floods potentially travel from the upper regions of the Darling River to their location hung in the air.

They decided to sleep on it, though little sleep was had. They were all a bit too spooked.

Dawn was breaking when Digger squirmed out of his sleeping bag on the floor and headed for the door, eager to discover what had landed in the billabong the night before.

Doc stirred and called out to him, "Wait a sec, Dig, I need to film this."

Jax and Mirren, not wanting to miss out, followed Doc to join Digger stretching outside. It was a cloudless sky, the air fresh, birds chirping; any sense of threat had vanished with the dawn.

As they walked, Mirren made a call on her satellite phone, arranging a meeting with her great-grandmother.

Digger, a bit ahead of the others and driven by curiosity, reached the bank and stood there, hat on, hands in pockets, staring at the brown water. Doc, filming closely behind, asked, "What do you see, Digger?"

"Muddy water," Digger shot back sarcastically. "Wait, there's something out there." He quickly stripped off his work boots and thick socks, wading into the water. Jax and Mirren flanked Doc, who continued filming.

"Be careful, Digger, it might drop off..." Mirren barely finished her sentence when Digger suddenly disappeared under the water, leaving his hat floating on the surface. Jax let out a yelp. The water stilled... they waited with worried looks on their faces. Doc kept the camera rolling, focusing on Digger's hat floating in the tranquil, muddy water.

Suddenly, like a submarine breaching the surface, Digger emerged from right under his hat. The others let out sighs of relief.

Digger guided a brown lump in the water towards the others standing on the bank. Once he was ankle-deep, he chuckled, "Dropped off a bit, eh?"

"Digger, what is that?" Jax asked, her expression turning into a frown.

"A big ole dead razorback … that's what plopped into the water last night. And, check this out," he said, dragging the large dead feral pig up onto the bank. "It's been gutted."

"Ew, how gross," Jax exclaimed.

Mirren, more accustomed to country life and unfazed by the gore, asked, "But how? And how could it have flown through the air and landed in the billabong?"

Doc, ceasing his filming, lowered the camera and said morosely, "Something big must have attacked it and tossed it into the waterhole."

# CHAPTER
# FOUR

Elsie Butler, the centenarian great-grandmother of Mirren, was gently rocking in her chair on the sunny veranda of her yellow Hardie plank bungalow on the outskirts of Leeton when they rolled up. It was boiling out—nearly forty degrees—and they could feel the heat hit them as they got out of the chilled Rav 4. The street was pretty, houses spread out with blooming jacarandas lining the way. Mirren led them up the path and onto the veranda, where she greeted Elsie with a warm hug and a kiss, then introduced the others.

"Help me up, girl. We'll go inside for some morning tea," Elsie suggested.

Digger licked his lips, already dreaming of hot buttered scones with strawberry jam. As Mirren helped her grandma past the group, Elsie teased Digger, "Ran out of strawberry, but I've got apricot." The fact that she had read his mind amazed Digger.

The living room walls were covered with Wiradjuri art—about fifty vibrant paintings that pulled Jax and Digger in like portals to the Dreaming. While Doc settled into a lounge chair, they stayed on their feet, mesmerised by the artwork.

"Mirren, there's tea and snacks in the kitchen on a tray ready to go," Elsie called out. As Mirren went to fetch it, Elsie shared with Jax and Digger, "It's the work of my family. One of them was painted by my mother in 1907. And that one," she pointed a bony finger, "painted earlier this year, is by Mirren's brother. We're originally Paakantji, from where the Paaka and Cooba rivers meet, up north."

Mirren came back with a tray from the kitchen and set it on the dining table, explaining, "The Paaka is the Darling River and the Cooba is the Murray River in our language."

"The Paakantji use circles and lines in their paintings to represent people and water," Elsie added.

Digger was drawn to one particular painting. "This one isn't using a circle or a line, is that a bunyip?"

Without even looking back at the painting Digger was referring to, Elsie said, "Sure is. You picked the one my mother painted in 1896."

"That was the year of the attack at Mont House," Jax noted.

"Was your mother here, I mean, in the area when that happened?" Digger asked.

"It was her brother with his woman and boy that were lost to the bunyip at the Mont House. I tell ya, that place is haunted by that thing… that's why it stays empty, no-one will go there. You kids are sure as hell crazy staying there … I told Mirren, didn't I? You best not do it if you care for your health."

"Do you think it's real or from the spirit world, Elsie?" Doc asked.

She paused, then answered gravely, "Both the same to me, both the same."

Doc managed a little filming, focusing on the paintings rather than Elsie, who preferred not to be on camera.

Back in the car, Jax brought up the earlier conversation. "What do we think about Elsie's warning?"

"Oh, don't worry about grandma, she gets a bit frantic about anything I get up to," Mirren dismissed lightly.

"I reckon the bunyip is just a big croc," Doc suggested.

Jax agreed, "Looked like one in that old painting."

"So, Doc, you reckon a big old croc gutted that razorback and hoisted it into the waterhole?" Digger challenged.

"I'm saying if you sum up all we now know, that's what it amounts to," Doc replied.

Mirren pulled into a parking spot outside the Stir Espresso Café on the main street of Leeton. "Dunno about you guys, but I could eat a horse and chase the rider … A friend of mine works here, and they do an all-day breakfast."

"Sold!" Digger said, hopping out first.

An hour later, their hunger sated, Mirren led them to the offices of Parks and Wildlife. In the boardroom, they discussed a plan that Doc had developed, with him standing next to a whiteboard jotting down bullet points.

"Okay, so in order of events we've experienced: first up, the razorback, mauled by something big and thrown through the air—let me point out that the animal would be at least the weight of an average man, so throwing it to the centre of the billabong was no mean feat. Second, we suspect an aquifer of an undetermined size underneath the billabong. Thirdly, a 19th-century Wiradjuri painting of a local scene at the time of the last known bunyip attack, depicts a large crocodile." He turned from the whiteboard to face them. "I propose we survey the billabong with magnetic resonance equipment and once assured of the size of the aquifer and its cave system and the safety, we scuba dive to explore it." Doc then took a seat to discuss his proposal further.

"What's that going to achieve other than putting the divers at risk?" Jax asked.

Doc answered, "It will eliminate that possibility to our investigation, Jax."

Jax nodded slowly, was satisfied with the answer.

"I know a drilling company in Narrandera that has an MRS..." Mirren started.

"MRS?" Jax queried.

"Sorry, it's a utility Geoscope... a magnetic resonance sounder. It's used for sourcing aquifers. I can arrange for them to come do scans, hopefully today. As for the scuba, I can arrange the gear from the Waterboard who use it for dam maintenance. How many would dive?"

Doc raised his hand, "I have a ticket."

Mirren could see Jax and Digger weren't certified. "I'm certified, so it'll be Doc and myself. All good."

"Mirren, do you think we'll get all this done in the time we have?" Jax asked.

"We just have to," Digger asserted.

Mirren nodded with determination. "We can only give it our best shot. I'll get onto Turner Mining and see if they have a Geoscope and operator available. The good thing is it reads out the results in real time on a digital display."

"Excellent," Doc said, clearly pumped about using some high-tech gear and diving into unknown waters.

Turned out there was a Geoscope being used by Turner Mining not too far away, and Mirren snagged it for them to meet at Mont House at 2 pm.

Next stop was the Leeton offices of New South Wales State Water. In the car, Mirren laid down some knowledge, "State Water controls the water coming from Burrinjuck and Blowering Dams in the Snowy Mountains into the Murrumbidgee River, which feeds the MIA, the Murrumbidgee Irrigation Area."

"So, they've got scuba gear?" Doc chimed in.

"Yeah, we team up a lot because they often find Aboriginal artefacts that we need to look after," Mirren explained.

"That's pretty cool," Jax said.

"The Murrumbidgee River was like a superhighway for the Wiradjuri people long before anyone else showed up. Gundagai, before all the settlers came, was this sacred spot for big meetings. And man, the weird stuff that's gone down there since—like a meteor lighting up the sky in 1876, a crazy storm dumping four inches of rain in two hours in 1885, and even a snowstorm in 1899 ... not to mention tornadoes, earth tremors, and in 1876, some wild electric fire-ball in the clouds that hit the earth and went boom! Plus, loads of lightning strikes over the years, way too many to just be random. But get this, the Murrumbidgee at the town of Gundagai, less than 200 kilometres from here, is famous for bunyip sightings. There's also this legend about the 'Mirriyolla Dog,' a spirit dog that can shape-shift. Oh, and the blue glow of Min Min lights, young Aboriginal children are taught to run if they see them."

"Whoa, it's like the ancient spirits are still fighting back against colonialism," Digger said.

"You really know your stuff," Jax noted.

"Ah, it's my gig. Plus, Gundagai's really close to my heart—it meant a lot to our people," Mirren shared.

They reached Mont House right as Jim from Turner Mining pulled up. Mirren knew him and quickly made the introductions.

"What are you using today, Jim?" Doc inquired, curious.

Bill, a rugged-looking guy around six-four, with ginger hair, a massive red beard, and notably large forearms, spoke in a gravelly voice, "A Numis MRS."

"How deep can it read?" Doc asked.

"Just over fifty metres. Should be plenty for what Mirren said you're looking for," Bill explained.

Jax jumped in, "How long to get a reading, Jim?"

"Fifteen minutes, it's pretty quick."

Not long after, they were on the bank of the billabong with Jim setting up the Numis unit. Digger stood beside Doc, watching Jim, and said conspiratorially, "Wonder what happened to the dead razorback?"

Doc looked around, "Yeah, I hadn't noticed, it's gone."

"If it hadn't, it would be pretty ripe by now. Something took it," Digger remarked, pulling a surprised expression.

"Okay," Jim announced, "I'll just float the transponder out to the deepest section, and we can get a reading." He gave the floating unit a push, watching it glide to the middle of the waterhole and stop right on cue. Jim, clearly skilled with the equipment, then walked over to the reader housed in a large case and looked at the screen. "See here."

They all crowded around Jim and peered over his shoulder at the screen.

Jim interpreted the readout, "Yep, there are two large caverns down there, and you can see a tunnel that probably leads off to Yanco Creek, judging by the direction. That second cave is the biggest I've seen in twenty years doing this. I'd say the first, smaller cave is underwater, but the big cave isn't. Anything else you wanna know, Mirren?"

"Can you tell if it's a running aquifer?" she asked.

"It sure is."

"Good, that means clear visibility down deep."

"Yep, you could definitely say that," Jim confirmed.

Doc, intrigued, asked, "You can't see if there are any anomalous live creatures down there, can you?"

Jim glanced at him as if he was crazy and chuckled, "Um, no."

# CHAPTER
# FIVE

An hour after Jim had packed up and left, Doc and Mirren were all suited up in scuba gear, ready to dive into the murky waters of the billabong. They were equipped with powerful dive torches, and both had safety lines clipped to their belts that Digger would manage from the shore. Before they popped on their face masks, they double-checked their single air tanks.

"Pity I haven't got an underwater housing for the camera," Doc told Mirren.

She held up a dive GoPro, "Got it covered, don't worry. For the first ten or fifteen metres, it'll be super murky," Mirren said, fixing the Go Pro camera to the rig on her shoulder. "But it should clear up once we hit the aquifer. I've done this kind of dive before, so just stick with me, okay?"

Doc nodded, his face a mix of excitement and nerves.

"Good luck," Jax called out, clearly impressed by their guts to dive into such spooky waters. The thought of what might be lurking down there, maybe even the beast that got the razorback, gave her chills.

Digger, handling the safety lines, gave Doc and then Mirren a reassuring handshake. His face showed he was worried, especially for Mirren. "Be careful, okay?" he said, his tone serious.

With a thumbs-up to each other, Doc and Mirren slipped their masks on and stepped back into the dark, brown water of the billabong, disappearing from view as they started their descent into the unknown.

The water was so murky that the torch light just made it worse. Mirren was right in front of Doc, but he could barely see her. A bit of sunlight managed to penetrate about a metre down, providing a ghostly ribbon of brown light. Doc had to rely on the buddy-line connecting them; it was comforting to know they were tethered together, especially with their two-way comms set up for cave diving.

"You okay?" Mirren's voice crackled through Doc ear bud.

"Yeah, hard to tell which way's up or down."

"It'll clear up, not far now."

Sure enough, a minute later they broke through to crystal clear water, like slicing through a murky ceiling into clear skies. The floor of the billabong was a whole other scene—covered in bones.

"This looks like a graveyard," Doc said with amazement.

"Plenty of animals fall into billabongs and drown," Mirren replied, calm as ever.

Right then, a massive black eel zipped between them.

"Whoa!" Doc yelped.

"Ha! That big old boy won't hurt you. This is his waterhole; he's just checking out the intruders."

Soon, they reached the source of the artesian spring.

"The water's changed temperature," Doc noted, feeling the warmth.

"It's the artesian spring. It's probably about 30 degrees," Mirren explained. "We need to go in here, through this cave mouth."

Mirren led the way into the metre-wide entrance.

Above water, Digger was carefully feeding the line to the divers while keeping an eye on their air bubbles. Suddenly, Jax noticed something.

"The bubbles stopped! What's happened?"

"It's okay," Digger responded calmly, still feeding the line. "It's still moving ... I guess they entered the aquifer."

Squeezing through the narrow entrance to the aquifer, Doc felt his tank snag on the edge. With a bit of a wiggle, he managed to free himself and followed Mirren into a tight tunnel. It was a tight fit, and the beam from Mirren's torch barely illuminated the four metres ahead. The water here was noticeably warmer, and Doc couldn't help but worry about the temperature rising the closer they got to the source.

Finally, they emerged into a large cave. The source of the aquifer was right there in front of them—bubbling away like a miniature orange volcano in the centre of the cave floor. It was a surreal sight. Mirren swam around the bubbling aquifer filming it. Across the cave, about ten metres away, her torch highlighted a shaft sloping upward at a 45-degree angle.

"Looks like that's the way to the second cave. It must be under the hill that's between the billabong and Yanco Creek," Mirren surmised, peering into the darkness.

"Let's move, it's getting too hot in here," Doc agreed, feeling the heat intensify.

Mirren led the way toward the dark shaft halfway up the cave wall, ready to explore the mysterious pathway that might connect to Yanco Creek. The adventure was heating up, both literally and metaphorically.

Digger was feeding the line when it abruptly stopped, then all of a sudden it pulled really hard dragging him off balance.

"Whoa! What was that?" he exclaimed, trying to stead himself.

Jax was concerned. Digger wound the handle on the winch to take up the slack but it didn't tighten. "Wait a minute that isn't right." He wound it harder and eventually they watched in horror as the end of the line came across the surface towards them. Digger held it up and with alarmed look of his face declared, "It's been cut by something."

Digger glanced at his watch again—an hour had passed since Doc and Mirren had submerged, and there was still no sign of them. "They'd be out of air by now," he muttered with a hint of despair.

Jax was on edge, biting her lip and pacing back and forth. "What can we do?" she asked, her voice tinged with helplessness.

"It'll be dark soon. We have to hope they made it to the big cavern and that it wasn't filled with water."

"Well, Jim figured it wasn't," Jax replied, trying to find some comfort in the facts they had. "So, you'd be right. If they're stuck anywhere, it would be in that cave. So, at what point do we panic and call a rescue team?"

"Soon," Digger intimated, nodding towards the setting sun. "It'll be dark in an hour."

The shadows from the surrounding trees were stretching across the glassy surface of the billabong like withered fingers. Jax and Digger were both weighing up the odds, pondering when to call for help. It would take the State Emergency Service in Leeton at least an hour to get there. First, they'd have to find divers, kit them up, and then drive them over.

"How long will their torches last?" Jax asked, trying to calculate their remaining window of safety.

"Five hours, but Mirren has a few flares. If they're stuck in the cavern, they could turn off one torch. That would double the time but for me that's not the problem."

Jax looked at him, wide-eyed and anxious. "No, then what is?"

"Whatever killed and ate that razorback could be down there, and we know it's only active at night." Digger's voice was heavy with worry, echoing the looming threat that now seemed all too real as darkness closed around them.

As the last traces of sunlight faded to a dim orange strip on the western horizon, the urgency to make a decision weighed heavily on Jax and Digger. Another half hour had slipped by—time was running out.

"I can't believe this is happening," Jax muttered, her voice laced with disbelief.

"I know, I know ... after all we went through in the jungles of Mindanao, here we are, in trouble right in our own backyard," Digger replied, equally frustrated.

Jax pulled out her phone, ready to call for help, but her frustration only grew as she discovered, "There's no signal!"

"You're kidding me," Digger said, pulling out his own phone only to find the same dead end. "I've got none either. Wait, Mirren has a satellite phone." He quickly rummaged through Mirren's kit-bag, relief washing over his face as he found it. "Ah, here it is." He flipped it open and started pressing buttons, then cursed, "Crap, it needs a password!"

They exchanged a look of despair, feeling the pressure mount as they scrambled for a solution.

"We've got no choice, one of us has to take the car and head towards town until there's a signal," Jax proposed, her voice steady despite the growing panic.

"You do it, Jax," Digger insisted firmly. "I'm not leaving you here alone in the dark."

"You sure? You're not armed or anything, what if...?"

"Don't worry," Digger interrupted, pulling a Bowie knife from the scabbard attached to his belt and holding it up so the last rays of sunset glinted off the big steel blade. "I've got protection."

Jax quickly grabbed the car keys from Mirren's bag and then gave Digger a reassuring hug before racing off towards the car, parked 100 metres away at the house.

Left alone, Digger tested the sharpness of his blade with his thumb, murmuring to himself, "I hope you're sharp enough to take out a bunyip, old son." His voice mixed hope with the heavy shadow of dread as he prepared for whatever the night might bring.

# CHAPTER SIX

Jax had barely reached the Rav 4 and was about to open the driver's side door when she heard Digger shouting, "Jax, come back!" Panicked, thinking something was wrong, she sprinted back as fast as she could.

Breathing hard, she found Digger not alone but with Doc and Mirren, alive and well. Overwhelmed with relief, she gasped, "God, I'm so glad you're okay ... I thought..."

Still in his wetsuit, Doc greeted her with a smile, "Wait till you see what we found!"

"Wait a minute," Jax panted after catching her breath, "did you swim out, or..."

"No, we found this massive grotto, and then a tunnel that led to Yanco Creek," Mirren explained.

"So we trudged back here from there," Doc added.

"Unbelievable," Jax exclaimed, still trying to process the news.

"You're not kidding, it's a labyrinth down there," Mirren remarked, eager to share the details. She quickly replayed the footage on the GoPro, providing a running commentary. "As you can see, the visibility was dreadful, then like magic, it cleared. See here the entrance to the artesian vent..."

"Wow, how narrow is that tunnel?" Jax interrupted.

"Yeah, I got my tank caught," Doc chuckled.

"We made it along the tunnel and here entered the cave containing the actual vent, see it..." Mirren continued.

"Looks like a volcano," Digger remarked.

"Then we spotted another tunnel ... so we entered it ... you can see it was again just big enough to fit us ... it was quite long but as we were going the water level dropped, see towards the end of it we were crawling in only six inches of water. Then, check this out ... we came to the edge of a cliff into a massive grotto. See as we shined our torches ... there's a rock pool in the middle and then around the floor are these..."

In the torchlight, the camera showed Aboriginal totems, six of them standing as they probably had for years.

"They are Jin!" Digger exclaimed.

"They must be ancient," Doc observed, suggesting the place was very sacred.

"No, it's not sacred," Digger corrected, "it's the ancient cave of a Marmoo! The totems are evil."

"I think one of them is Gugaa, the totem of the Wiradjuri. We need to show this to Elsie ... she's best to interpret the totems," Mirren suggested.

They were all aghast; the footage was amazing.

"So, what are we thinking?" Jax proposed.

"Well, we now know the tunnels connect, so a croc could make it all the way here from the upper reaches of the Darling," Doc noted.

"Yes," Mirren agreed, "and we also need to acknowledge there could be a spiritual connection to the cave, one that might conjure something to protect the sacred site."

"That makes sense," Digger agreed.

"Both make sense, Digger," Jax corrected. "But which is correct? Which was responsible for the murders back in 1907?"

"Not forgetting the razorback," Digger added.

Realising they were standing around the billabong with only torchlight in the night, feeling vulnerable, they collectively decided to pack up and get the heck out of there.

They quickly dropped off the scuba gear and then drove straight to Elsie Butler's place. When they walked into her living room, they found her chilling and watching TV.

Elsie looked up with a friendly smile, "Television shows just aren't what they used to be."

Mirren sat on the arm of Elsie's recliner, holding her hand. "Too right, Grandma. We've come to show you something interesting."

"Oh, good ... have you guys been chasing that bunyip again? I hope you haven't caught it and brought it here," Elsie joked, glancing around as if expecting to see it hiding somewhere.

"No, no ... Doc's got a video to show you. We went scuba diving in the billabong at Mont House today," Mirren explained.

"Hey Elsie," Doc said, starting the GoPro footage from when they entered the grotto.

"Is that down there? My goodness," Elsie remarked as she watched.

"See here, these totems?" Mirren pointed out.

"Ah yes, that one is Gugaa, the Wiradjuri totem ... they're very ancient. Wait..." Elsie's expression changed, and she shivered. "Those other totems are Jin!"

Digger gave Jax a look—he'd said the same thing about them.

With a serious look, Elsie warned them, "This is the cave of the bunyip. You've stirred up some real trouble, girl ... The Jin totems were placed there to keep it locked up. By taking someone from outside the Wiradjuri there, you've broken the spell."

"But how does that explain the last attacks in 1896?" Digger asked, intrigued.

Elsie locked eyes with him, her voice grave, "Sometimes the cave entrance gets exposed. Someone must've gone in and broken the seal."

"Can we fix it?" Jax jumped in, clearly worried.

"I don't know how," Elsie admitted, looking uneasy. "But the last time it was broken, it took three sacrifices before the bunyip had its fill."

They all took in the heavy news, realising the gravity of what they might have unleashed.

As they drove back to Mont House, the car was filled with their intense conversation about the mysterious events.

"That doesn't explain the recent cattle mutilation and the razorback," Doc pointed out, still sceptical of the supernatural explanation.

"Maybe it was like Grandma said, at times when Yanco Creek is low enough the entrance to the grotto gets exposed, as we witnessed ourselves," Mirren proposed, trying to piece together the puzzle.

"But Elsie said someone had to release it by going there," Digger added, highlighting a key detail.

"Well, maybe someone did … kids … a fisherman … a prospector…?" Mirren suggested, thinking of possible culprits.

"True, we'd never know unless someone had reported it or had been attacked," Jax offered, considering the likelihood of unnoticed interference.

Mirren confirmed, "None of that has happened."

Digger then chimed in with a practical suggestion, "First thing we should do tomorrow is seal up the Yanco Creek entrance."

"First thing we need to do is find out how to fix the broken spell," Jax corrected, focusing on the root of the problem.

"I think we need to find a Garratji," Mirren suggested, bringing up a potential solution.

"What's that?" Jax asked, unfamiliar with the term.

"A Wiradjuri medicine man that deals with evil spirits," Mirren explained.

They devised a plan that tackled both the supernatural and the natural explanations for the disturbances at Mont House. Mirren took on the task of connecting with the Wiradjuri community. She would ask Elsie to help her get in touch with the elders, hoping they could introduce her to a Garratji, a Wiradjuri medicine man skilled in dealing with evil spirits.

Meanwhile, Doc, still not entirely convinced about the supernatural angle and decided to explore the possibility of a large crocodile lurking in the area. He planned to set up a few baits around Yanco Creek and the billabong to test his theory. Mirren supported his approach by providing him with nocturnal sensor game cameras to capture whatever might be drawn to the baits. She swung by her office to pick up two camera setups and then hit a nearby supermarket to buy four full roast-ready chickens for bait.

Just as they pulled up at Mont House, Mirren received a text inviting her to meet with Wiradjuri elders at midday in Gundagai. She quickly arranged for the Parks and Wildlife helicopter to pick her and one other person from Mont House at 10 am to attend the meeting. It was decided that Digger would go with her, given his vested interest in the outcome, while Jax would stay behind to assist Doc with the data collection from the game cameras.

After a quick meal, it was time for them to venture into the night to strategically place the baits and set up the cameras.

It was 10 pm, and the last quarter moon peeked out through clouds scudding across the night sky as they gathered on the porch. They divided into two teams: Jax and Digger to place two chicken baits and a camera by the billabong, and Doc and Mirren to set up their equipment by the Yanco Creek exit of the grotto.

Equipped with torches, each team headed towards their designated objectives. Jax and Digger reached the billabong, and while flashing the torch along the bank, Jax suggested, "Maybe by the reeds?"

"Yep, there's a willow for the camera," Digger agreed.

In one hand, Jax carried a plastic bag containing two chickens, and in the other, two metal spikes to tether them. Digger reached up, clamped the camera on a lower branch of the large willow tree, and aimed it where Jax was tethering the chickens.

The silence was unnerving, devoid of the usual nocturnal chorus of frogs and crickets. "It's all a bit too quiet, don't you think?" Digger remarked after finishing with the camera mount.

Jax folded her arms and shivered, not from the cold but from the eeriness. "Yeah, let's get back to the house; this place freaks me out."

Suddenly, a loud rustle came from nearby bushes, causing them both to flinch. They flashed their torches towards the sound, but nothing appeared. Jax whispered fearfully, "What was that?"

"I dunno, but maybe the smell of the dead meat is attracting something. Let's get out of here," Digger replied.

They hurried towards the path to Mont House.

Meanwhile, Doc and Mirren were navigating through a thicket of trees leading to the hill. The sound of Yanco Creek running on the other side of the hill guided them. Mirren, walking behind Doc, noticed something. "The bag you're holding is leaking, Doc."

He stopped and checked. "Thawing out, I suppose, just a dribble of chicken juice."

"We don't want anything picking up the scent while we've got it," Mirren cautioned.

"True, we're nearly there," Doc responded as they continued.

# CHAPTER
# SEVEN

As Digger and Jax were rushing from the thicket surrounding the billabong across the field towards the house, Jax stopped abruptly and called out, "Digger, Digger! There's something following us!"

Digger stopped. "Where?"

Jax aimed her torch back at the trees and spotted a pair of red eyes glaring at them. "There."

Digger, pointing his torch towards the eyes, drew his Bowie knife and took a few steps forward.

"No, Digger!" Jax appealed. "It's big; a knife will be no use."

The creature moved slowly through the long grass. Digger paused with his torch fixed on it. "It's a wombat, Jax."

"What if it eats the chicken?"

"They don't eat meat; it's a whatchamacallit, um, a vegan," Digger joked.

"Herbivore," Jax corrected.

"Yep, that's it."

Meanwhile, Mirren had her torch on Doc's hands as he tethered the chickens to the muddy bank at the mouth of the grotto exit. After finishing, he shone his torchlight on Mirren fixing the camera to a lower branch of a gum tree overhanging the fast-moving creek.

"I wonder how often the creek completely dries up?" Doc mused quietly.

"More often since the Burrinjuck and Blowering Dams were built in the Snowy Mountains," Mirren said from up in the tree.

"When was that?"

"They started on the Burrinjuck in 1907, finished it in 1926. The Blowering was built in the 60s," Mirren informed. As she was getting down from the tree her foot skidded on the trunk and the torch slipped out of her hand. It hit the ground and went out.

Doc picked it up and flicked the switch, "Busted, no worries, we've still got mine." He gave Mirren a hand down. "You know, I don't think it's more than a coincidence that in the same year they started building Burrinjuck Dam, the attack happened here. The first thing they would've done is divert the Murrumbidgee River, which would've quickly dried up Yanco Creek."

"And exposed the entrance to the grotto for the first time to the colonists."

"Exactly. I reckon Mont found it but didn't report it."

"Otherwise, even in those days, it would've been declared a sacred site and that would've meant losing land," Mirren explained. "He might've broken the seal."

"Or, when the creek dried up, a big old croc living in the grotto needed to go looking for tucker."

Just as he finished speaking, a low guttural growl came from the bush behind them. Doc aimed his torch in that direction. Something was there—waiting—watching them.

Jax had Mirren's laptop open for her and Digger to check the game camera at the billabong. It was working fine; when sensor activated it would send pictures via a satellite cellphone connect to the laptop. It had been activated once since they'd set it up. They watched a rabbit hop past the chickens, its eyes glowing in the infrared light.

While they were having a chuckle about the rabbit, an alert popped up that Camera 2 was online. "No pictures yet, it hasn't been triggered."

"Can you activate it from here?" Digger asked.

Jax hit the space-bar, and they got a picture. "There you go, two dead chickens."

"Can you turn up the sound?"

"I think so, um." The dropdown menu had sound, she clicked it and then increased the volume. They could clearly hear babbling Yanco Creek. Then they heard a loud growl and a voice call out, 'Mirren, quick!'

Jax looked sharply at Digger and shrieked, "That was Doc! Sounds like they're in trouble!"

Doc was leading Mirren at speed, following the beam of his torch through the thick undergrowth. A vine whipped across his face, and then whack, he ran into a thick branch—the torch flew out of his hand, hit the ground hard, and flicked off, and so did he— Doc was out cold—Mirren was left standing frozen in the darkness.

"Doc, Doc?" Mirren whispered urgently... But there was no response. Feeling her way through the bush like a blind person, moonlight suddenly broke through the clouds enough for her to sight Doc on the ground. She knelt down beside him. Then she heard the chilling growl of whatever was following them. It was close.

A loud rustle came from the bushes ... she looked sharply behind her expecting to see a crocodile or a bunyip, but instead she saw the flash of a torchlight and to her relief the sound of Digger's voice, "Mirren, Mirren is that you?"

Doc woke up with a throbbing headache and puzzled over how he'd ended up back at the house. Mirren updated him: Jax and Digger had assisted her in carrying him home.

"Did any of you catch a glimpse of what was lurking in the bushes?" Doc inquired, nursing a coffee.

"No, but we all heard it," Digger replied.

Mirren booted up her laptop and announced, "Well, well, we got two hits." They eagerly huddled around her to view the recordings. Camera 1 by the billabong captured a large goanna seizing a chicken and, shaking it vigorously like a dog, dragged it into the underbrush. The next four activations revealed nothing—likely just owls or smaller creatures.

The fifth activation caught a young fox stealthily entering the frame. With its eyes aglow, it snatched a chicken leg and swiftly disappeared.

After a quiet spell, at dawn, a majestic wedge tail eagle swooped down and effortlessly carried off the remnants of the chicken. They switched to camera 2. The first trigger showed a large black eel struggling comically to snatch one of the chickens, eliciting laughter from the group as it retreated back into the creek, visibly disappointed. The subsequent activation displayed only a few yabbies nibbling at the chicken remains.

"Could those yabbies have set it off?" Digger wondered.

Mirren shook her head, "Doubtful, they're too small. There must be something else nearby."

"Boost the audio," Digger suggested.

Upon enhancing the sound, they distinctly heard something rustling through the foliage accompanied by a deep growl.

"A dingo, perhaps?" Mirren speculated.

Then, a sudden blur of brown whisked both chickens out of sight.

"Holy mackerel! What was that?" Mirren exclaimed.

"Rewind and slow it down," Doc suggested.

Mirren complied, but they could discern only a blur. They reclined in their chairs, contemplative, until Doc broke the silence. "Whatever darted into the frame was enormous…"

"And to snatch both chickens in one go," Digger noted.

Doc stood, resolute, "It must've been a croc."

"I'm not sure, given its proximity to the creek, it might have been a massive Murray Cod—known to drag live sheep into the water," Mirren countered.

"I'm still betting on a croc," Doc maintained.

Jax, lost in thought, suddenly spoke up, "There's one way to find out."

"Go on," Digger encouraged.

"Set a trap. If it's a croc with an appetite, we should be able to catch it," Jax concluded.

The chopper swung by at 10 am, ready to cart Mirren and Digger off to Gundagai to chat with some Wiradjuri elders and hopefully meet a Garratji, a medicine man. Meanwhile, Jax and Doc watched the chopper lift off, then jumped into the Rav 4 for a trip to the Parks and Wildlife office in Leeton. Mirren had set them up to meet with James Close, her senior field officer, to sort out a plan for making a crocodile trap.

James, a tall, skinny guy with a wild beard, was super chill and really helpful. He liked to be called Jim and showed them around the big workshop at the back of the facility.

"We can definitely build a trap with the specs from Wildlife up in the Northern Territory," Jim said.

"I bet they deal with crocs more than you guys do," Doc remarked.

"For sure. I've been around the Murray and Darling rivers for twenty-two years and never bumped into one myself. Oh, wait—I remember someone found a croc skeleton and some skin up near Macca's Beach on the Murrumbidgee after the last big flood."

"Yeah, Mirren mentioned that," Jax chimed in.

Doc was all in on that info, "That pretty much seals it that crocs can make it down here."

"Seems like it," Jim agreed, all laid-back. "Might even explain some of those weird cattle mutilations going on around here lately."

Doc shot Jax a quick 'told ya so' look.

Since Gundagai doesn't have its own airport, they landed the helicopter at Gundagai District Hospital. Elders Cody Walker and Jean Simpson were there to meet them. With pilot Rick Malone, they drove into Gundagai town, parking right outside the Niagara Café on the quiet main drag, Sheridan Street.

"Is the statue of the dog on the tuckerbox on this street?" Digger asked, stepping out of the car.

Cody grinned, his voice rough like gravel. "Nah, easy mistake. It's at Snake Gully, eight clicks out. But hey, this café here, the Niagara? It's the oldest Greek milk bar in the country, been around since 1902."

Rick hung back to chill in the café's outdoor seating while Mirren and Digger headed inside.

"Niagara's a quirky name for a café in Gundagai, right?" Digger said.

"Maybe after the big waterfall near Talbingo on the Tumut River, about an hour from here," Mirren suggested, always ready to drop some local knowledge.

They joined Cody at a booth, and the whole gang settled in. The café still rocked some of those art deco vibes, kinda like those old-school American movie theatres from the '30s. A few other folks were around, grabbing coffee and an early lunch.

Jean asked, "What's your mob, Digger?"

"Yidinji, up north of Cairns."

"That's a fair trek from here," Cody noted. "Might be the first meet-up for our mobs."

"What's the scoop on the Garratji man we're meeting?" Mirren asked.

Jean explained, "A Garratji man's like a spirit catcher from way up in the gulf. Here, our medicine man's called a Bunjin. Our guy, Birrani…"

"Birrani means 'boy' in Wiradjuri. He's a healer and a spirit medium, does some serious magic," Mirren filled in for Digger.

Just then, a shadow fell over their table, thick with presence. Digger glanced around for the source but came up empty. Turning back, a voice broke the silence.

"Welcome to Wiradjuri country of the Dharawal mob."

Digger looked back up, and as if out of thin air, there was this guy in his forties, salt-and-pepper hair in a ponytail, and a beard to match, sporting a red shoulder bag. He squeezed in opposite Digger and Mirren.

Offering a hand Digger said, "Name's Digger of the Yidinji mob."

Birrani shook, then took Mirren's hand and said knowingly, "You are kin of Elsie Butler?"

Taking it in her stride, Mirren replied, "Yep, she sends her best wishes."

His eyes sparkled as he looked at Digger, "A coffee would go down well."

Digger chuckled, expecting maybe something a bit more mystical, and waved over the waitress.

Birrani listened intently as Mirren explained the situation at Mont House. Their coffees arrived just as she was finishing. They waited for Birrani's assessment.

"The place you describe on the Yanco is ancient and serves to contain a Bugin spirit. The Buin were malevolent medicine men of the Dulu-durrai from Dulu, up where the Marrambidya meets the Barka—white man calls these rivers the Murrumbidgee and Darling. The Bugin could shape-shift to attack or escape its pursuers. From what you say, one must have been caught there. Under certain circumstances, it can be freed from its lair, but only at night; sunlight will destroy it."

# CHAPTER EIGHT

Later that afternoon at Mont House, Mirren retold the story to Jax and Doc.

"So, let me get this straight," Jax began, "Birrani believes the Bugin was trapped in the grotto by Wiradjuri totems, but it can be freed temporarily by someone not of the Wiradjuri, allowing it to shape-shift into the bunyip and feed on people."

"Yes, that about sums it up," Mirren confirmed.

"You know what? I think the bunyip is just a crocodile," Doc declared emphatically.

"Did he tell us how to defeat it?" Jax asked Digger and Mirren.

"Yes, there are specific rituals to lure it out of the grotto at night, then use items that will prevent it from returning to its lair, and sunlight will do the rest," Digger explained.

Mirren added, "Effectively vaporising it."

"Ah, come on, pull the other one, vaporises? Like a vampire in some B-grade horror flick," Doc scoffed. "It's all mumbo jumbo."

Mirren stood with her hands on her hips, giving Doc a stern look. Jax intervened before the situation escalated. "Don't worry about Doc, Mirren. Just let him do his thing, and we'll do ours."

Doc stormed out of the house.

Digger joined Doc on the porch steps, the mid-afternoon sun beating down on them. "A coldie would go down well right now," Digger remarked, peering out from under the brim of his hat.

"Too right … So while I'm setting up a croc trap, you guys will be having a corroboree?"

Digger chuckled. "Ha! Something like that."

Mirren's voice shouted from inside, "Can you guys go and retrieve the game cameras?"

"On it," Digger called back.

By the time Digger and Doc returned to the house, Jim was waiting by his tray-back truck. Doc approached him and introduced Digger. "Been here long?" Doc asked.

"Nah, turned up five minutes ago."

Doc handed Digger the game camera. "Drop these inside, mate. I'll give Jim a hand. Oh, could you bring me back my camera?"

The cage on the tray was three metres long, but the two of them easily lifted it off and placed it on the ground. Digger returned and handed over the camcorder. "Mind if I get this?" Doc asked.

"Fine," Jim acknowledged, then explained to the camera like a true professional, "It's best to place the trap on the bank of the creek overnight. To set it, lift the hatch, place the carcass inside, right down in the middle. The croc will go inside, and the hatch will snap shut—it can't back out so it'll be secure. It'll thrash around trying to escape but if you stake it down well, it'll eventually give up and fall asleep." He went to the truck cabin and returned with a large heavy-duty plastic bag. "Here's half a sheep, should be enough. When you check it at dawn, if you've caught anything, give me a ring ... I'll be here in twenty minutes. All good?"

"Yep, all good," Doc confirmed.

Jim shook hands with both men and said, "Good hunting."

"Well, Digger," Doc said watching the truck drive off, "you'll need to give me a hand to get this thing into position before we lose the light."

The ugliest part of the whole ordeal of setting the croc trap was loading in the rotting half carcass of a sheep for bait. It was seriously foul-smelling. Both guys washed their hands in Yanco Creek afterwards.

"I can't get the smell out of my nose ... I can taste it," Doc complained.

"Mate, the stinkier it is, the better our chances of attracting a croc. Are you happy with the position now?"

"Yep, let's just check the stakes once more; we don't want it escaping."

They gave each of the four metal stakes an extra tap with the mallet Jim had left, just to be sure. As the last embers of daylight flickered in the western sky, they headed back to the house.

Doc was surprised to find Jax and Mirren close to naked, their bodies adorned with white paint. Digger began stripping off to be painted in ceremonial paint as well.

"Let me get this on video; it's too good to miss," Doc said, raising the camcorder.

Doc was asleep when a rhythmic clicking sound woke him. He went to the front door and peered out. The sound was coming from the billabong; he knew it was Digger, Jax, and Mirren performing the ceremonial dance the medicine man had advocated. He ducked back inside, grabbed the camcorder, and headed off to capture the event.

Filming all the way, when he reached the billabong, he found the two girls dancing around a small fire, clicking sticks in time, while Digger was at the water's edge, throwing items into the middle of the pond. The girls' bare feet kicked up dust into the glow of the fire, and the mantra they were chanting in unison was monotonous and heady. They paid no attention to Doc, as though they were in a trance.

Digger cast a final item out into the pond and, chanting the mantra, joined the dance. His expression was one of intense focus, as if he were in a trance or mesmerized.

The sound of their combined voices seemed to Doc to hum and pulse with nature, even the crickets and frogs appeared to harmonize. The fire flickered out, and they stopped abruptly as if a switch had been flicked. He had no idea how long they had been performing the ritual, but it seemed to be over. Still in a trance, they walked off single file back towards the house. Doc followed, filming. It felt as though he had been witnessing an ancient ceremony, and he was glad he'd captured it.

Strangely, as soon as they set foot inside the house, they snapped out of their trance. The three painted youths looked at Doc with mystified expressions on their faces.

"Wow, that's insane," Jax mumbled, checking the time on her phone. "Three hours have gone since we painted up here, and I remember none of it."

"Same here," Digger said.

"Me too," agreed Mirren.

"Lucky I got it on video," Doc chimed in.

While the girls washed off their body paint and changed, Digger sat on the floor deep in thought. Doc sat beside him.

"I feel really weird," Digger admitted.

"Like what?"

"I don't know, like I'm out of my body ... stoned ... no, no, more like I'm connecting with something or someone that I don't know. Yes, that's it," he said animatedly, "it's like when we did pituri back in Sydney and connected to the Dreaming, only whatever we just did, I still feel connected to it somehow."

"Yeah well, that's creepy. Think it's the same for the girls?"

"Might be," he said vaguely.

The girls returned from changing, so Doc asked, "Digger's feeling a bit strange. What about you two?"

They both sat on the floor next to the guys. "We were just talking about it," Jax said. "Mirren's more affected than me, but yes, we feel like we opened the door to something dark and then left it open."

"Yeah, that's a good way of explaining it," Mirren agreed.

Doc rolled out his sleeping bag. "Well, I'm going to hit the hay. I've got to get up at dawn to check the croc trap."

Mirren got up and locked the front door, while Jax lit a few more candles, as the others had burned down.

All nestled in their sleeping bags, Doc asked sleepily, "Is that all you had to do with the ceremony and all?"

"No," Digger said with a sleepy groan. "The ritual should have woken up the bunyip. It should be out now, hunting."

Doc sat bolt upright in shock. "Hunting! Like what?"

"We don't know, we have to go to the exit by Yanco Creek, just before dawn to place a magic bullroarer just inside the cave entrance."

"And what's that supposed to do?" Doc asked.

"It closes the spell so the bunyip can't return to its lair," Mirren answered.

Doc questioned further, "What's to stop it from returning through the billabong?"

"I had to throw seven objects Birrani gave us into the water to seal it off."

"Yeah, I filmed you doing that."

"Good. I wasn't sure I'd done it."

"What's to stop it from coming here and attacking us?" Doc asked.

"I just hung a charm on the door handle; it won't come in here," Mirren said confidently.

Jax said after a yawn, "Let's hope Birrani knew what he was talking about ... I set an alarm for 5 am; sunrise is at 6:30. That'll give us time... Goodnight."

They all curled up in their sleeping bags, Doc thinking of a croc taking the bait, the others thinking of the bunyip.

# CHAPTER NINE

Jax woke with a fright. The candles had burnt out and the room was pitch black. She rolled to the side and checked her phone for the time; it was 3 am. The screen light woke Digger.

He whispered, so as not to wake the others, "What is it, Jax?"

"I don't know, I think a noise woke me."

They both struggled out of their sleeping bags, went to the front window, and peered through the wooden slats of the shutters. A light breeze blew through, stirring their hair—there was no glass.

"I can't see anything out there," Digger mumbled.

Beside him, Jax agreed, "Me either."

Suddenly, two reptilian hands burst through the shutters without breaking them, and two clawed hands grabbed Jax by the face. Digger quickly drew his Bowie knife and struck with all his might at the two forearms, but the blade passed right through them as if they weren't there. Struggling in a frenzy, Jax managed to wrench herself free. A head passed right through the shutters and snarled at them. It was seriously ugly, with large reptilian yellow eyes, scales covering its skin, long, pointed teeth like needles. No ears, just wart-like bumps all over its head and face. In place of hair, a fin with short sharp spikes. It was horrific—Jax was frozen with fear. Digger quickly grabbed the bullroarer from under his bedroll and held it up like a crucifix to a vampire. The creature hissed like an agitated big cat and then withdrew. Jax was holding her chest, trying to calm her pounding heart. Digger stood facing the window, frozen, the bullroarer held out in front of him.

Doc stirred, looked up, and when he saw the two of them standing there in the dark like that, asked, "What the heck are you two doing?"

Mirren sat up, awakened by Doc's voice. "What is it?"

"Something just came through the window and attacked me," Jax said, panting as if she had run a marathon. "I think it was the bunyip."

Doc got up and inspected the window, which was intact. "How? There's nothing…"

"It materialised right through the shutters," Digger explained. "Its claws ... it grabbed Jax by the face ... I tried to cut her free, but my blade passed through its arms like they weren't there. Then, it stuck its head through ... it looked seriously wrong ... the bullroarer stopped it ... it backed out and took off."

Doc shook his head disbelievingly and, while getting back into his sleeping bag, said, "I think you're both delusional after the ceremony."

Digger dug into the red cloth bag Birrani had given him and took out four small painted river stones.

Propping himself up on his elbow, Doc asked, "More mumbo jumbo?"

"Protection," Digger replied as he went to place a stone at the rear door and the other three at the windows.

"You should respect what Digger is doing, Doc. It's for your protection too," Mirren said.

Jax turned off the alarm; she hadn't really needed to set it. None of them got any more sleep since the incident. Jax, Digger, and Mirren kept thinking every shadow and every sound was the bunyip, and Doc thought the same of a crocodile. They all got out of their sleeping bags in silence. Digger went out onto the front veranda and stood looking into the night as though something was out there looking back at him.

Doc ambled out and joined him. "Mate, sorry for being the cynic. It comes with the way I think. Sometimes opinions are better left unsaid."

"No, Doc, I understand why you think the way you do. Someone has to, it's important. There's no need to apologise, man."

They both fell silent, listening to the sounds of the night.

Doc cracked the silence, "So, you have to put something from your red bag of tricks at the entrance to the grotto. Is that to stop it entering or leaving?"

"Both. If it's in there, the seal that was broken is reset. If it's out, then it won't be able to enter and will be destroyed by the sunlight."

"So it can't get out through the billabong?"

"No, not after I threw those charms into the water."

Doc raised the camcorder. "Let's get on film what you've got in the bag."

Digger flicked on the torch he was holding, then drew a bullroarer out of the bag, holding it in the light so the camera could pick it up in detail. "This is a bullroarer. The Wiradjuri medicine man Birrani we consulted about the bunyip hand-painted it with sacred symbols to ward off the evil spirit of the bunyip."

Doc zoomed in for a close-up of the shaped slat of wood. "It's thirty centimetres long by five centimetres wide, painted as you can see with white dots and dashes, with cord wound around one end. One edge has been sharpened so when it's swung in a large circle in a horizontal plane, the aerodynamics cause it to spin, producing a vibrato sound. Bullroarers have been used for thousands of years by my people to communicate and to ward off evil spirits. They are considered secret men's business by all or almost all Aboriginal tribal groups, and are forbidden for women, children, non-initiated men, or outsiders to even hear. This one was cut by Birrani from a sacred tree in Wiradjuri country."

Mirren and Jax joined the guys on the veranda. Doc stopped filming and Digger looped the bag over his shoulder.

"Let's go," Mirren said.

Holding the bullroarer ready to swing it if needed, Digger led them towards Yanco Creek. Everything seemed normal until they reached the thicket of trees flanking the creek. Quite suddenly, the birds that had been singing praises to the coming dawn stopped their song, as if nature itself had held its breath. This meant something more to Digger, Jax, and Mirren than to Doc, who carried on, seemingly unaware, the other three now on high alert. Fifty metres from the creek, the trap, and the cave entrance, Digger threw up his hand, signalling them to stop; something was rustling through the undergrowth ahead. Knowing the bunyip needed to reach its lair before sunrise to survive, Digger knew he needed to get there first.

He said, "Doc, lead the girls to the trap, I'm going ahead to the cave entrance."

Jax was about to protest, but Mirren grabbed her arm and gave her a look that silenced her.

Digger moved off into the bushes that quickly enveloped him. Doc continued on cautiously with the girls following close behind, all their nerves on edge.

Digger stopped in the thick of the bushes and closed his eyes. He tried to connect with his surroundings, hoping he might be able to sense the presence of the bunyip. The sound of a light breeze rustled the leaves above, but there was no breeze—only the stillness that comes just before dawn. He had tapped into the Dreaming and felt connected to every living thing around him. He could sense the location of Doc and the girls, he could not only hear but feel the running water of Yanco Creek—he sharply opened his eyes; he could also sense the presence of evil.

Realising it was a race between him and the bunyip to reach the cave entrance first, Digger tapped into the adrenaline rush of fear and bolted through the tangled brush.

Doc stepped into the clearing by the creek and flashed his torch along the water's edge, hunting for the trap.

"See it?" Mirren whispered.

"Nope, thought it was right here," Doc muttered, his light sweeping back and forth.

"Everything looks different at night ... I think the cave entrance is like twenty metres down," Mirren guessed.

"Alright, let's keep tracking the creek then. Watch your step though, it's slippery here," Doc advised.

"I keep picturing a croc leaping out of the water with those massive jaws," Jax said, her hushed voice edgy.

"Same here," Doc agreed in a low voice, his torchlight leading the way along the precarious bank.

Without using his torch, Digger reached the bank of Yanco Creek. Moving along it, guided by instinct alone, he suddenly stopped when he heard a noise ahead. Thinking the bunyip was beating him to the cave entrance, he pulled out his torch and shone it towards the sound—two beady red eyes lit up, staring back at him from just three metres away, right on the edge of the water. He cautiously moved toward the eyes, hoping his torch beam would reveal more. Is it the bunyip? he wondered. Or a croc?

It moved, and the torchlight revealed it was actually a sixty-centimetre platypus, a big female, beside what he figured was the entrance to her nest, probably protecting her eggs. Relieved, he skirted around the burrow, realising it had probably been the platypus he'd heard earlier. Platypuses often scavenge for food on land at night.

As Doc rounded a small bend in the creek, his torchlight caught a sinister gleam off something metallic. Approaching cautiously, he recognised it as the trap. He stopped, turned to the girls, and whispered in a tense voice, "The trap is just ahead. Wait here while I make sure it's safe."

Jax flicked on her torch, her voice trembling slightly, "I'm not staying here in the dark."

Doc edged toward the trap, his torch sweeping the murky surroundings to ensure no croc was lurking nearby. The beam suddenly revealed an unexpected sight.

# CHAPTER TEN

The trap was shut, triggered, but eerily empty—not even the half of a sheep's carcass remained.

"Girls," Doc called back, his voice tinged with confusion, "All clear, but … it's weird."

Mirren appeared first, with Jax close behind, their torches darting nervously through the shadows.

"Did you…?" Mirren's voice trailed off as she caught sight of the empty trap. "No luck, huh?"

"Look at this—the trap was triggered ... whatever did it took the bait, literally."

"Far out," Jax whispered, her tone a mix of disbelief and fear, while Doc captured their bewildered expressions on his camcorder.

Suddenly, a loud clunk echoed through the trees. Doc's heart raced as he swung the camcorder and torch towards the sound. The trio froze, their hearts pounding, half-expecting the grotesque sight of the bunyip or a colossal crocodile. Instead, they saw Digger standing there, his hands and the knees of his army fatigues caked with mud.

"Digger!" Jax gasped, relief flooding her voice.

"You're looking a bit worse for wear," Mirren observed, eyeing his muddy appearance.

"That's what crawling through a tunnel on all fours in twenty centimetres of putrid mud does for you," Digger replied, his voice weary.

"The water level must've dropped since we last swam out," Mirren noted, thoughtfully.

"See anything?" Jax asked, her voice still edged with concern.

"Nope, just the biggest platypus I've ever seen, and honestly, it looked more terrified than me."

"Where did you place the bullroarer?" Mirren inquired, her tone serious.

"Birrani instructed to put it about three metres up the tunnel from the creek," Digger explained, gesturing vaguely towards the dark place he'd emerged from.

"Well, we didn't have any luck," Doc said, panning the camera and torchlight around the empty trap.

"What happened? Where's the bait?" Digger exclaimed.

"Not only is it gone, but the trap's been triggered. How does something get in, trip the trap, and then get away with the bait, leaving it set off?" Doc mused, puzzled.

"See any prints on the ground around it?" Digger asked, shining his torch on the ground.

"Nothing," Mirren said, looking around bewildered.

"Unless it was the bunyip," Jax suggested. "We know it came right through the shutters at the house ... so it could just reach in and drag the bait out."

"Yeah, if it did that, the bait would trip the trap on the way out," Digger added, nodding.

Doc turned off the camcorder and lowered it. "Come on, that's like saying aliens beamed it up."

"Hadn't thought of that," Jax said with a facetious smirk.

Mirren looked east and announced, "Sun's coming up. That ends the photo op with either critter."

"True," Jax said tiredly. "Let's head back to the ranch. I could murder a hot coffee."

Digger led the way back to the house, all of them relieved the night was over but dissatisfied with the results. As they emerged from the trees into the field, daylight had fully broken. Kookaburras laughed and magpies warbled under the cloudless blue sky.

Jax inhaled the fresh country air, aware that by evening she, Digger, and Doc would be back in the big smoke, where the air was far less crisp. She took hold of Mirren's arm as they walked. "I'm going to miss you, Miss Butler."

"Yes, I've grown quite fond of you lot as well," Mirren admitted.

"Ever come to Sydney?"

"Oh, once in a while for conventions and stuff."

"Well, if you do, stay with me … and if you're ever in need of a job change, yell out. We could do with someone of your talents at the Next Files."

"Ta, Jax."

Jax looked over her shoulder at Doc, who was trailing and filming them. She gave the camera a big smile and said, "So, all's well that ends well."

Digger reached the veranda of the house first and was going up the four stairs when he stopped and yelled out, "What the…!"

The others caught up with Digger and stopped, staring down at what had him transfixed. At the front door lay the grotesque sight of half a sheep's carcass—the bait from the trap.

They all exchanged totally puzzled looks.

They had all been deep in thought while packing up their belongings and walked in silence to the car. The image of the sheep carcass lingered in their minds, unresolved and haunting.

It wasn't until Mont House had disappeared behind the dusty trail of the Rav 4 that Jax finally spoke up. "Well, let's hear it … who's got an explanation?"

Digger was the first to respond. "Unexplainable, I think that's what it is. I'd like to believe the bunyip took the bait out and dropped it on the doorstep as a message, and that when the sun came up it was vaporised."

"Or it took the carcass while we were heading for it, dropped it off, and then made it back into its lair before you placed the bullroarer to stop it ever getting out again," Mirren offered.

"For me, both of those scenarios are implausible," Doc countered. "I just don't see a creature like Jax described, spiritual or physical, taking the bait, tiptoeing through the forest, dumping it on the doorstep, and darting off, having a good laugh. A bunyip with a sense of humour? No, something else … like, someone playing a prank on us."

"What about how this all started … cattle mutilations," Digger brought up.

"Are you suggesting aliens, Digger?" Doc asked sceptically.

"Seriously, how else can you explain the trap being set off with the bait gone and it ending up on the front doorstep, huh?" Digger argued. "It's either alien or spiritual ... your theory about a big croc is totally blown out of the water, Doc. No croc could have done it."

"I agree with Digger. I know what I saw. Whatever came through the window and grabbed my face was intelligent, I could see it in its eyes," Jax chimed in.

As they hit the bitumen road, the cabin quieted, filled only with their thoughts until Mirren broke the silence. "There's one other possibility; a Dooligah."

"What the heck's a Dooligah?" Jax inquired.

"A creature from Aboriginal folklore," Mirren explained. "Mostly found on the south coast, from Narooma through to Eden. The Yuin mob there speak of it, and there have been sightings in that region and in the Snowy Mountains over recent years."

"You talking about a Yowie?" Digger queried.

"Yep, standing about 5' 6" to 5' 9", hairy like a gorilla, Australia's answer to Big Foot, Yeti, Sasquatch, the Abominable Snowman."

"No, I'm less inclined to believe that than the bunyip. Has such a creature ever been sighted around here?" Doc questioned.

Mirren explained, "National Parks and Wildlife were contacted in January 2021 about a Yowie sighting at Pine Island on the Murrumbidgee River near Tuggeranong. There were plenty of sightings during the big bushfires of 2019, the fires flush them out."

"Do Parks and Wildlife confirm their existence?" Doc asked.

"They neither confirm nor deny. But one thing that might suggest we've been dealing with one is Aboriginal folklore says the Dooligah is an intelligent creature and a known trickster. That might explain the carcass on the doorstep," Mirren concluded as she pulled up at Narrandera airport.

They got out of the car, just in time for the flight to Sydney, departing in fifteen minutes. Doc gave Mirren a hug. "Your explanation makes sense, Mirren, but I'm afraid for me this one will remain non liquet. Good to know you and thanks for everything, tell Jim about the trap, that should tickle his fancy."

"I will, Doc," Mirren replied with a big smile, appreciating his scientific approach despite their differing views.

Jax was next, giving Mirren a big hug, then holding her at arm's length with tears in her eyes. "Umm, I'm going to miss you.

I'll send you a file link to the story once it's cut. Don't forget what I said about coming to Sydney and the job."

Mirren could only nod, tearing up as well. Then came Digger. His hug carried more emotion than the others, and Mirren felt it. They kissed, a friendly goodbye kiss. Digger was lost for words, and so was Mirren, but they both felt a special chemistry. Just as Digger was about to move off, Mirren grabbed him by the arm, pulled him into an embrace, and kissed him passionately.

Digger stared out the airplane window at Mirren standing alone in the airport car park, looking pretty downcast.

Next to him, Jax nudged him playfully. "She's totally perfect for you, bro."

"You think?" Digger muttered, sounding a bit gloomy.

"I know so, and deep down, you do too. Don't chicken out on this. I offered her a job with us … it's a real shot for you guys to be together."

Digger chewed on his bottom lip and sighed. "Ah man, I don't know. I've got so much baggage…"

"Digger, come on. The only way to deal with that sort of baggage it to unpack it and wear the responsibility. If you've got issues, get some help … but seriously, a girl like Mirren is rare. Don't let her slip by."

Digger gave Jax's knee a thankful pat. Across the aisle, Doc was busy charming a pretty stewardess who was handing him a coffee. Jax rolled her eyes and whispered, "Doc's such a flirt."

"You might wanna follow your own advice, sis," Digger shot back with a teasing grin.

# CHAPTER ELEVEN

It was Anzac Day, so the ride from Sydney domestic airport was slow, the roads choked with traffic. But the delay hardly mattered; the radio in the black SUV that picked them up was playing "Parallel Worlds" by Two-Up, stirring different memories for each of them.

For Doc, it was about his dad; a session guitarist who had played with Two-Up. He remembered the stories his dad shared about recording sessions with the band. Digger was taken back to the protest rallies in Queensland where he'd stood against mining companies. There, 'Parallel Worlds' became an anthem, blaring from loudspeakers, embodying the struggle of the little guy against the corporate giants. Jax recalled her parents in their Manila apartment, the track a staple on their Aussie protest song compilation CD, dancing through the living room with youthful abandon.

You're not so different
Just you and I have
Opposite views

Your nuclear vision
Your plan of fission
Might be right for you

I believe in a safe world
At the moment
You pose a threat

Parallel Worlds
Parallel Worlds
Parallel Worlds
Parallel Worlds

You can't convince me
Your talk of peace
Is as thin as ice

It's wishful thinking
To think that bombs
Are a peacekeeping device

I believe in a safe would
I can feel that you
Need the threat

Parallel Worlds
Parallel Worlds
Parallel Worlds
Parallel Worlds

One, two, three, four
We don't want nuclear war
Five, six, seven, eight
We don't want to radiate!

One, two, three, four
We don't want nuclear war
Five, six, seven, eight
We don't want to radiate!
Parallel Worlds
You're caught in
Parallel Worlds

As they absorbed the lyrics, the contrasts struck Digger—the words of the song juxtaposed against the sights of people gathering to commemorate Anzac Day. It all made sense to him, the notion that we live in parallel worlds, perhaps more now than when the song was released back in 1983. That was a time marked by nuclear tensions, not with Iran and Israel, but with Russia following the downing of Korean Airlines flight 007 over Soviet airspace. He recalled reading about the near-miss with nuclear war when a Soviet early-warning system falsely reported the launch of an American Minuteman ICBM. Diplomats had scrambled to prevent retaliation, a story of a crisis averted by the thinnest of margins. The ongoing threat of nuclear war, Digger remembered, had been a recurring shadow since 1956, a dark cloud returning every couple of years.

As the song faded out, the weight of these thoughts seemed to lift slightly, yet the significance of their meanings lingered in the quiet that followed.

As they arrived at the office, Doc wrapped them both in a quick hug before jumping in a taxi to head home. Digger and Jax headed inside to catch up with Janet. But no sooner had they walked through the door than they were greeted by the cheerful sight of Tilly. The big-hearted lady nearly sprinted across the open-plan area to envelop them in a massive hug. After a brief chat about her extended stay with the Santos family in Davao, Jax and Digger proceeded to Janet's office to discuss the outcome of the bunyip adventure.

The briefing with Janet lasted about twenty minutes and ended with her looking somewhat disappointed.

"I love the Blair Witch Project vibe with Doc capturing it all, but what I don't like is having no outcome ... We can't keep leaving the audience hanging," Janet expressed.

"I get that, but isn't it the nature of these unexplained events to be left open to interpretation?" Jax countered.

"Don't overestimate your audience, Jax. Plenty of shows have tanked doing that. It's a rule of thumb to give the audience closure ... otherwise, you're just making a doc for the History Channel," Janet argued.

Digger then chimed in with a suggestion, "What if we re-create what Jax saw at the window and label it 're-enactment'?"

"You mean a guy in a rubber suit?" Janet asked, not quite convinced.

"This is the entertainment business, isn't it?" Digger said, leaning back, comfortable with the idea.

"We could do that, it wouldn't be hard to re-enact, and I can play the part of myself," Jax added.

"And I'll get in a latex suit," Digger said, chuckling.

"Done!" Janet declared with a huge smile. "Now, go tell Carter that, because he's worried the story doesn't have a happy ending too."

Minutes later, they pitched the idea to Carter. They waited nervously for his reaction as he swivelled in his chair, flicking a pen between his fingers. Finally, he stopped, glanced at them one by one, then cracked a massive smile. "Bloody brilliant! Who came up with the bunyip at the window?"

"It was Digger, boss," Jax admitted.

"I knew you were more than just a pretty face, Digger. Good stuff. Right, you guys get on with that … I assume this time Doc kept the footage and didn't drop it in Yanco Creek."

"All's good," Digger confirmed.

"The Lang Suyar story rated well, Jax … I'm keen to see how 'Blood of the Aztecs' rates next week. We've spent heaps on CGA to recreate the lost city. Thank Janet for that."

"Can't wait to see it," Jax said, sharing an excited glance with Digger.

"The best news is … North America and the UK have picked up the series," he announced, beaming. "That means season one is locked in, and I'd say season two will be as well. Congratulations, Jax. There will be a party tonight in your honour after the preview of 'Blood of the Aztecs'. You guys up for that?"

Jax was too busy blushing to respond, so Digger answered for her, "Too right. Does Doc know?"

"He would by now."

Janet had taken over the 'Friend in Hand' pub for a private party, arranging for 'The Time Benders' to play a live set and setting up a screen and digital projector for the exclusive preview of "The Next Files," episode 4, "Blood of the Aztecs."

Jax arrived solo and was warmly welcomed at the door by Julie, a junior staff member from NewsLine. Inside, the venue was buzzing with about thirty of NewsLine's staff, Janet's production and post-production crew, and a few higher-ups from the television station whom Jax hadn't yet met.

As soon as Carter spotted her, he whisked her away to meet the network executives, including Tony Cornish, the international sales agent responsible for the North American and UK deals for "The Next Files."

Not long after, Digger and Tilly made their entrance and were quickly introduced to the executives as well. Jax and Digger enjoyed engaging feedback from Tony, who shared enthusiastic responses from overseas screenings of the first three episodes.

Carter drifted over to their group, and Jax remarked, "No speeches, huh? Looks like everyone knows what we're celebrating, no need for any long-winded talks."

Carter replied with a grin, "No problem, if that's what you want."

Just then, Digger noticed Beano, the front-of-house engineer, stepping behind the mixing console. "There's Beano, the band's coming on."

"Aren't you playing?" Jax asked, a hint of tease in her voice.

"It's just one set. If they need me, they'll give me a shout, but I didn't bring my didge tonight."

As the band launched into their first song, "Foul Play," Doc made his way to the centre stage with his guitar, stepping up to the microphone to sing, capturing the crowd's attention.

Seems the higher we climb
The farther we fall
There's sharks and cheats
fists banging at the door

The world's going rotten
Yeah, it's rotten to the core
The powers that be
Wanna start another war

And I, can't buy believing
In what the bigshots say
Battered 'n bruised by the fake news

I've got no time (no time)
No time for foul play

Talking about the crime
While riding on the line
Biting on a cheese burger
Sucking up the slime
The prophets that be
They deliver no sign
But some time baby
We'll be travelling in time

But I, can't buy believing
In what the bigshots say
I'm battered 'n bruised by the fake news
I've got no time (no time)
No time for foul ....

But I, can't buy believing
In what the bigshots say
I'm battered 'n bruised by the fake news
I've got no time (no time)
No time for foul play

Guitar solo

But I, can't buy believing
In what the bigshots say
I'm battered 'n bruised by the fake news
I've got no time (no time)
No time for foul...

That's why I, can't buy believing
In what the bigshots say
I'm battered 'n bruised by the fake news
I've got no time (no time)
No time for foul play (fake news)
No time for foul play (fake news)
No time for foul play

The performance unfolded in the explosive, engaging manner Jax and Digger had come to expect—the audience was thoroughly captivated. Just before the last song, Doc addressed the crowd with a heartfelt introduction.

"I work with an extraordinary woman … I've got to say, I've never met anyone quite like her. She's not only drop-dead gorgeous, but she also thinks right out of the box. She's a pocket-rocket, there's no-one braver. Tonight, we're here to celebrate the success of her television series 'The Next Files.' Now, it takes more than one person to create a TV show, and I know she acknowledges her producer Janet, the crew, and our boss, Des Carter … I'm speaking for her here because one of her most endearing qualities is her humbleness. It's cute…"

A facetious murmur rippled through the crowd. "Okay, okay, I'll admit I'm fond of her … So, alongside her through thick and thin is her brother, Digger, a guy cut from the same block of granite. So, as much as she'll loathe me for it, come up here Jax, and bring that brother of yours with you."

Her face flushed a bright red, Jax took Digger's hand, and he led her through the applauding crowd onto the stage. They received a warm reception.

"Folks, give it up for Jax De Loite," Doc announced.

Jax stepped up to the microphone, cleared her throat, and said, "Thank you, Doc. And let me say, while Digger might be on my left, my right-hand man is Doc. He is the rock-solid foundation our show is built on, and I can't thank him enough. He's much more than a great singer and guitarist—please give him a big hand."

The audience responded enthusiastically. Now relaxed, Jax continued to express her gratitude to the members of NewsLine and of course, acknowledged her brother. After she finished, Doc took over.

'Stay here and join us, you two, for the last song of the night, 'Somewhere in my Mind.'"

After the song, Doc led Jax and Digger off the stage while Beano and a roadie lowered the screen for the premiere of "Blood of the Aztecs."

Jax, Digger, and Doc were thrilled by the standing ovation the show received at its conclusion. Des Carter took to the stage and expressed his gratitude on behalf of NewsLine. The night had exceeded everyone's expectations.

Backstage with the band, Doc introduced Beano, the band's sound engineer, to Jax and Digger.

"Want a drink, Beano? I need a top-up," Doc offered.

"No, Doc, I'm going to split. I've got to leave the load-out to Mullet; I've got a late-night recording session."

"Oh? Who are you recording?"

"Mixing a track for the death metal band 'Carnage Asylum'," Beano replied.

Beano, an Indigenous man in his early 20s, stood at about 5' 8". Skinny and unshaven, he had the archetypal look of a rock engineer/producer. His long black hair, sharp, intelligent eyes, and a gruff smoker's voice—though he probably only smoked weed—along with his obligatory uniform of black jeans, a black AC/DC T-shirt, and an oversized black denim jacket gave him an unmistakable presence.

"Wow, that'll be heavy on the ears," Digger remarked.

"Too true, especially since it's a midnight to dawn session. But I'll be on my own, so I can keep the monitors low to minimise ear fatigue."

"Which studio, man?" Digger inquired.

"I was going to do it at home using Pro Tools, but the band insisted on an analogue mix, so it's at Atomic, a little studio in Surry Hills, not far from NewsLine."

"Cool, I live not far from there. I pass it on my way home. So, what's the track so I can keep an ear out for it?" Digger asked.

"It's 'Hellhouse.' Originally released by the Perth metal band Black Alice in the early '80s. Carnage covered it in their inimitable style. Drop in and have a listen if you're a night owl."

Digger shook his hand. "Might just take you up on that, Beano."

# HELLHOUSE

# CHAPTER ONE

(Intro)
If you're looking for a thrill or two
I've got a place for you
to chill you through.
They say Satan walks the floors at night.
Waiting for someone to feed his appetite.

If you're game enough to take the risk
Not afraid to taste the devil's kiss
Understand you're a better man than I,
Go and look Satan square in the eye...

Hellhouse, hellhouse
666 Dead End street
Hellhouse, hellhouse,
where the centre of the earth
and the surface meet.

(solo)

Folks tell of sulphureous smells
of death and decay
If you end up with the walking dead
then you're there to stay.

No-one returns to tell
of what's inside
It might be paradise,
it might be fire...

666 Dead End Street
Hellhouse, hellhouse,
Hellhouse, hellhouse,
666 Dead End Street
where the centre of the earth
and the surface meet.

(middle 8)

If you're game enough to take the risk
Not afraid to taste the devils kiss
Understand you're a better man than I,
Go and look Satan square in the eye...

Hellhouse, hellhouse
666 Dead End Street
Hellhouse, hellhouse,
Where the centre of the earth
and the surface meet.

Hellhouse, hellhouse
666 Dead End Street
Hellhouse, hellhouse,
Where the centre of the earth
and the surface meet.

Beano had just finished listening through a rough mix of 'Hellhouse,' checking out the lyrics on his screen, when his phone pinged with a text. It was from Skull Duggery, the lead singer of Carnage Asylum. He had sent over two audio files to add to their song 'Hellhouse,' with specific instructions.

Beano opened his laptop and located the two files labelled '1' and '2,' accompanied by a note: 'Beano, file 1 goes over the intro, file 2 goes over the middle 8. I want them backwards. Whatever you do DON'T play them together, they're separate for a reason. Skull.' The capitalized 'DON'T' was impossible to miss. Amused, Beano was well aware of Skull Duggery's reputation for pranks, as legendary as his stage name suggested.

Driven by curiosity, Beano transferred the files to the main computer and, despite the warning, queued up both files on the same timeline. A deep, frightening, demonic voice boomed through the studio's large monitors, uttering unintelligible, bizarre words that sounded to Beano like Latin. He chuckled at Skull's diabolical creativity and, ignoring the explicit warning, flipped the vocals to play them backwards.

As soon as the eerie backward vocals began, the studio lights started to flicker wildly. The temperature in the room plummeted, sending a chill down his spine and causing the hairs on his neck to stand on end. The unsettling words from the track echoed in his head, repeating over and over as if stuck on a loop. He clapped his hands over his ears and slammed down the faders to silence it, but the haunting voice persisted.

Standing up, his face contorted in distress, hands still pressed firmly over his ears, Beano caught his reflection in the large studio window. But instead of his own reflection, he saw a ghoulish face peering back at him, straight out of a horror movie—glaring yellow goat's eyes with black lids, wickedly sharp teeth, and skin the sickly grey of a corpse. His heart raced as panic set in, "Is that me? Who are you!" he shouted, backing away from the console, struggling to catch his breath and desperate to figure out how to halt the nightmare he'd unwittingly unleashed.

Digger pulled up outside the Newtown terrace where he, Tilly, and Doc lived. He left the engine running as Tilly and Doc prepared to hop out.

"Aren't you coming in, mate?" Doc asked, pausing in the doorway of the car.

"Nah, I'm wide awake. Think I'll drop in on Beano at Atomic Studio, check out 'Hellhouse'," Digger replied, his decision firm.

"Man, that's not the kind of music you want to be listening to at this hour. Good luck with that," Doc chuckled, stepping out of the car.

Digger nodded and drove off, the quiet streets of the city unfolding before him.

He parked in front of the studio. The tree-lined street was deserted, save for a black cat darting across—the sudden howl of a distant dog pierced the eerie silence that 3 a.m. typically brought to the city. However, none of this fazed Digger. Having starred in the premiere of "Blood of the Aztecs" earlier and survived genuinely terrifying ordeals, including the recent bunyip case, he had become considerably toughened. An empty city street, a howling dog, and the anticipation of a tumbleweed rolling by weren't going to unsettle him. He marched up to the front door and pressed the buzzer as if everything was perfectly normal.

When no answer came, Digger figured Beano might not have heard the buzzer over the music he was mixing, so he pressed it again. Still no response. He tried the door, and it swung open. Shrugging, he stepped inside. The lights were off, but a sliver of light under a door at the end of the corridor caught his eye. Assuming it was the studio because of the music emanating from that direction, he headed towards it. As he approached, the strains of 'Hellhouse' grew louder; he opened the thick studio door, and the music hit him full force. Just inside, to the left, was a small band room equipped with a coffee machine, a pool table, and a bar fridge. He called out towards the control room, trying not to interrupt, "Beano, you there? It's Digger." With no reply, he stepped into the control room. He could see Beano's back, seated at the recording desk, engulfed in the blaring sound from the big studio monitors.

Digger approached Beano and tapped him gently on the shoulder. When he got no response, a sinking feeling prompted him to turn the chair around. To his horror, it wasn't Beano slumped in the chair but a security guard, dead with gaping black holes where his eyes should have been, blood streaming down his cheeks, his face frozen in a grimace of terror, and his shirt stained deep red. Digger recoiled, his heart pounding as he frantically scanned the room for any sign of the perpetrator.

Within fifteen minutes, Atomic Studios was teeming with police—uniforms, detectives, and forensics swarmed the area, transforming it into a hectic crime scene, with Digger as a suspect.

Bathed in the flashing blue lights of the cop cars, Digger stood outside the studio, answering questions from Detective Inspector Rick Malone, when Jax arrived, ducking under the police tape.

"This is a crime scene, miss," Malone stated gruffly.

"And he's my brother. He phoned me," Jax shot back, her concern evident. "What's happening, Digger?"

"I came to see Beano, but found a murdered security guard instead," Digger explained. "I was just telling DI Malone here..."

"He says he works for you at NewsLine, miss?" Malone interjected, his rugged demeanour suggesting time experienced in the poolhalls of life.

"Sorry, Jax de Loite. Yes, we produce a show called—"

"The Next Files, yeah, I know. That episode, Min Min, didn't exactly flatter the police," he growled in his deep, gravelly voice.

"Hmm, we'll be more mindful of sensitivities in the future," Jax offered an apologetic smile.

Malone's gaze hardened on Digger. "Okay, de Loite, you're free to go, but stay within city limits."

As dawn crept in, Digger led Jax to his car and paused. "There's a café down the street about to open. Fancy a coffee?"

Jax nodded, and they walked off together, leaving the chaos of the crime scene behind.

Over caramel lattes at the café, Jax pressed Digger for details. "His eyes had, like, exploded—it was super gross ... like his head had imploded."

"What the heck could do that? And where's Beano? Think he's okay? Maybe we should call Doc for his number?" Jax pondered.

Digger glanced at the wall clock. "Good idea, though I doubt he'll appreciate a call at 6 a.m."

Too late—Jax was already dialling.

Twenty minutes later, Doc joined them, nursing a Voodoo X coffee, renowned for its potent caffeine punch. After getting briefed on the grim details, he tried calling Beano but only reached his voicemail.

"Where does he live?" Digger inquired.

"He's got this quirky place he inherited over in Hunters Hill. I dropped him off there once after a gig," Doc explained.

"We better check it out," Jax said, her voice tinged with concern.

"Did you say the guard's eyes had exploded?" Doc asked, eyebrows raised.

"Yep, insane ... DI Malone couldn't believe it either. But the forensics expert mentioned he bled out big time, massive brain damage, blood from the ears ... all that ... Maybe Beano is a Yara-ma-yha-who?"

"A what?" Doc looked puzzled.

"Yara-ma-yha-who, a freaky creature from the Dreaming. Gets inside people's heads," Digger explained.

Jax was already on her phone, looking it up. "Here it says, the Yara-ma-yha-who is this little red dude, kind of like a frog with a massive head, no teeth, and suckers on his hands and feet. Hangs out in fig trees and sucks the blood out of folks chilling underneath. Then he swallows them, has a drink, takes a nap, and spits them back out a bit shorter and redder. Do it enough times, and bam, you turn into one."

"That seems a bit far off, doesn't it?" Digger admitted.

"Look, I've known Beano since we were kids. He's no monster out of some horror flick," Doc reassured them, standing up. "You guys up for heading over to Hunters Hill to see if he's alright?"

# CHAPTER TWO

Digger, sitting in the passenger seat, mused aloud as they navigated the morning rush hour traffic, "Why would Beano bail out of the studio leaving everything on and the song playing?"

"Maybe whatever got the guard frightened him off ... it would've me," Doc replied, his eyes focused on the road.

"Then why was the guard in Beano's chair?" Digger pressed on, not quite satisfied with the explanation.

"Now that is weird," Jax chimed in from the back seat.

"Seriously," Doc agreed.

What was normally a twenty-minute drive had turned into a forty-five-minute crawl due to traffic. Eventually, Doc pulled up in front of an old two-story house just a few doors down from the Hunters Hill Hotel.

"How old is this place?" Jax asked, peering up at the house through the car window.

"I think he once told me like 1880. Belonged to his great uncle," Doc said as he opened the car door.

The brownstone terraced house, crowned with two reddish spires, was shrouded by huge, dark green fig trees that cast long, thin shadows over it, giving it a sinister appearance.

"Looks creepy," Digger noted as he climbed out of the car.

Doc creaked open the old front gate. The path to the house was overgrown with grass and weeds. "Lawn hasn't been mowed in ages," Digger observed.

Doc chuckled. "Beano's about as far from the lawn-mowing type as you can get."

They walked up the four steps onto the veranda. While Doc went to the door and knocked, Jax whispered to Digger, "Wouldn't live here for anything."

Digger was eyeing a crow perched on the front fence, watching them. "Me neither, even that crow looks wicked."

Doc knocked a second time with no response. He then turned to the others, bending down to lift a flowerpot by the door and pulling out a key from underneath. "Aha!" he exclaimed, fitting the key into the lock and pushing the door open. "Always amazes me how folks hide keys in such obvious places."

Jax and Digger joined him at the doorway. "Should we be doing this?" Jax questioned.

"Too late," Digger said, following Doc inside.

A narrow hallway opened up into a living room that flowed into a dining room and then the kitchen. Doc, assuming the bedrooms were upstairs, called out, "Beano, you there, mate? It's Doc!" The place had that lived-in vibe: open pizza boxes on the coffee table, an Aboriginal flag proudly displayed on one wall. Along another wall stood a bookcase brimming with books, Blu-rays, and vinyl records. The centrepiece was an elaborate home entertainment system featuring a Marantz amplifier, cable set-top box, turntable, cassette and CD players, among other tech. At the room's end, a 70-inch flat screen TV, surrounded by an 8:1 speaker setup, took pride of place. Walls adorned with posters of famous progressive rock albums completed the scene.

"This guy totally lives and breathes music and film," Digger said, awestruck by the collection.

Jax pointed at a four-seater couch. "There's the jacket he was wearing last night at the gig; he must be here somewhere."

Just then, the floorboards creaked, and Jax looked up to see Doc heading up the stairs.

"This place would be worth a fortune," Digger remarked, settling into one of the lounge chairs as light streamed through the window, illuminating the dust motes dancing in the beam.

"Probably a heritage site," Jax commented, "but definitely needs a vacuum." She wandered over to the turntable, spotting a vinyl record on it. Picking up the sleeve, she read, "Dead O Deluxe by Carnage Asylum." She flipped it over. "Wow, check out the lead singer, Skull Duggery," she said, walking over to Digger and handing him the album. Skull's face was covered in tattoos and piercings, his head bald, and his ears sculpted to points. The other band members sported long hair, looking far less intimidating than Skull.

"Produced by Beano. Wouldn't want to meet Skull on a dark night … Check out some of these song titles: 'Necrophilia,' 'Autopsy Love,' 'Gut Full of Dreams…'" Digger chuckled. "Memorable."

Upstairs, Doc reached the landing and paused, surveying the hallway bathed in beams of dusty sunlight. With three doors on either side, he figured one was a bathroom and the others bedrooms. He opted for what seemed like the main bedroom door, opening it gently. "It's Doc, Beano, you there?" he announced softly, not wanting to startle anyone.

The room was dim, blinds drawn, with a double bed where he could just make out the shape of someone under the covers. Clothes were strewn over a chair. Recalling Digger's harrowing description of the dead security guard, Doc moved closer, hesitantly reaching out to tap what he presumed was the shoulder of the curled-up body under the covers. He nearly jumped out of his skin when the figure stiffened and then sat up sharply—a young girl with a shock of curly black hair, her eyes wide with fright.

Quickly, Doc put a finger to his lips. "Shush, don't scream, it's okay, I'm a friend of Beano's … My name is Doc. So sorry to wake you." He managed to calm her down; she leaned over and turned on a light. Now he could see she was about sixteen, rubbing her eyes and blinking to bring him into focus.

"What's going on? Hey, I know you. You're the lead singer of the Time Benders."

"Yeah, sorry to scare you, but I need to see Beano urgently."

"I didn't hear him come in … He usually gets back from Atomic in the mornings and then crashes. His room is next door. What time is it?"

"Just gone 8," Doc answered.

"Uh, must've missed the alarm, need to get ready for school," she said, hopping out of bed. In her flimsy nightdress, with bare feet peeking out, she was undeniably pretty. "I'm Bindi … Beano's my cousin."

Doc gave her a warm smile. "Sorry again for frightening you, Bindi."

"Hey, it's cool, I would've slept in. Go wake Beano up..."

Doc left Bindi's room and went next door, pushing open the door gently. "Hey Beano, you there, mate? It's Doc." A groan responded from the darkness.

Meanwhile, Jax had put the album cover back on the turntable and resumed her seat on the lounge. As she did so, Beano's jacket slid off onto the floor. Picking it up, she noticed blood on it. Just then, Bindi, now dressed in her school uniform, came tearing down the stairs, seemingly running late, and darted out the front door. Jax froze, holding up Beano's jacket, and exchanged a mystified glance with Digger. "Who the heck was that?" she exclaimed, startled.

Digger was just as puzzled. "I've got no idea."

Jax turned her attention back to the jacket. "Look here, there's blood on Beano's jacket."

Before Digger could reply, they heard another creak from the stairs and saw Doc descending.

"Who was that?" Jax called out to him.

"Who?"

"A girl in a school uniform just flew out of here like the place was on fire," Jax explained.

"Oh, that must've been Bindi, Beano's cousin. I woke her up; she was running late for school," Doc clarified.

"Did you find Beano?" Digger inquired as Doc settled into a lounge chair with a heavy sigh.

"Yep, he was asleep ... He's getting dressed, should be down in a minute."

Jax stood up, still holding the jacket. "I'll go make some coffee."

"Good thinking," Doc nodded.

"Check this out, there's blood on Beano's jacket," Digger mentioned, handing it over to Doc.

He sighed. "Argh, we better get this to forensics ... Beano will need to hope it's not from the security guard," Doc mused.

They all looked up as Beano made his way down the stairs. He looked tired and dishevelled, as if he'd had a rough night with little sleep. His body language was heavy as he sat on the lounge and ran his hands through his thick, curly black hair in despair.

Doc held up the jacket. "This yours, mate?"

Beano looked up, his eyes bloodshot, and nodded. "Yeah."

"It's got blood on it. Look, last night Digger went to Atomic to meet you and found a dead security guard," Doc explained.

Unable to meet their eyes, Beano muttered, "All I remember is playing back the track 'Hellhouse' a bunch of times, doing some trims and adding in some effects Skull had emailed me ... then it all goes blank. The next thing I knew was you waking me up."

"It doesn't look good, Beano. You bailed out of the studio, left the track playing, and everything on," Doc pointed out, his tone grave.

Digger chimed in, his voice equally serious, "And there was a dead guard in your chair, his eyes blown out, plus there's blood on your jacket."

Finally making eye contact, Beano's expression crumbled, tears starting to well up in his big brown eyes. "You've gotta believe me, guys ... I don't remember anything. I don't even remember seeing Ralph, the security guard. He makes his rounds daily at exactly 3:00 AM. What time did you get there, Digger?"

"It had just gone 3 AM," Digger replied.

"So that adds up," Beano said, his mind racing as he tried to piece things together. "I got there around 1 AM. So, when did I leave? I know, the CCTV will tell us."

# CHAPTER THREE

While Beano was upstairs grabbing his bag, Jax was carefully packing his denim jacket into a plastic bag to hand over to the police. Doc and Digger stood by, ready to head out.

"Looks like you might have given us a new Next File, huh, Doc?" Digger half-joked, trying to lighten the mood.

"I wouldn't be so sure. I think there'll be a logical explanation for all this," Doc replied, always the rational one.

Jax shot him a sceptical look with one raided eyebrow. "Heard that before."

Soon, the four of them were seated around a board table at the Homicide Division, waiting for Detective Inspector Malone. Doc noticed Beano shifting uncomfortably in his seat and tried to reassure him, "Relax, mate. You've got nothing to hide. You'll be fine."

Beano gave a nod, but it was clear he wasn't convinced.

DI Malone entered the room, remaining standing with an air of impatience. When he spoke, his words came out rushed, as if he didn't want to waste a minute. "The CCTV shows you leaving in a hurry at 2:47 am. Why were you in such a rush, Beano?"

"I don't know, I can't remember," Beano responded, his voice uneasy.

"That's convenient," Malone quipped sarcastically.

Doc, looking to clarify the timeline, asked, "Did the CCTV show the guard entering?"

Malone didn't seem pleased with the question. He paused before replying, "2:57."

"He makes his rounds at 3 every morning," Beano pointed out.

"And me?" Digger asked, curious about his own appearance on the footage.

"3:04," Malone answered dismissively. He then outlined the next steps, "Here's what's going to happen. You're going to leave Mr Beano Walker here with me to answer some questions. He'll text you if and when he'll be released." With that, Malone headed for the door.

"Am I under arrest? Do I need a lawyer?" Beano called after him.

Malone stopped at the door, turning back with a grim look. "I'd get one if I were you ... and make sure they're good."

Their exchanged glances were filled with concern. Malone's parting words did not sound at all encouraging.

Outside Central Police Station, walking to their car, Jax could sense Doc's deep thought and nudged him, "You're quiet, what's going on in that hard-boiled brain of yours?"

"None of this adds up, that's what," Doc replied, his brow furrowed. "Like Beano leaves Atomic at 2:47... Ralph arrives ten minutes later, then seven minutes after that, you show up, Digger. So, Ralph gets there after Beano has left, and during those seven minutes before you arrive, he gets his eyeballs blown out ... and you don't see anyone come out of the joint."

"So, whoever killed Ralph had to still be there when you showed up. How long before the cops arrived?" Jax pondered.

Digger thought for a second, "About 15 minutes, pretty quick ... Central's just up the road."

"During the time you waited, did you stay in the control room?" Doc asked.

"No, it was too gruesome, I went out the front and phoned the cops ... and waited there."

"Is there a rear door?" Jax queried.

"No, but there's an upstairs attic. I know because they keep master tapes there. It has pull-down stairs in the band room," Doc explained.

They stopped at the car. "You thinking whoever killed Ralph might have gone into the attic?" Jax asked, piecing it together.

"Had to be," Doc concluded. "If it wasn't Beano, and the CCTV showed no-one else coming out, it's the only place the killer could've been…"

"Wonder if the cops searched it?" Digger mused. "Maybe they didn't know its there."

Doc opened the car door but before getting in, he added, "Maybe not. I think we better take a look ourselves."

Before starting the car, Doc decided to call Cindy Blue, the owner of Atomic Studios, to get a handle on the studio's schedule for the day. Cindy shared that the studio was currently being cleaned in preparation for a session scheduled at midday. That session would wrap up by 6 p.m., and almost immediately afterward, at 6:15 p.m., she had planned a recording lesson for students from the nearby Sydney High School.

"How long will that last?" Doc asked, thinking ahead.

"Until about 7:30," Cindy replied. She added that nothing was booked after that—it was supposed to be Beano's time to finish the mix of Hellhouse for Carnage Asylum.

Doc seized the opportunity and booked the studio for an hour starting at 7:30 p.m. Cindy, curious, asked about Beano and what Doc thought of the whole terrible incident.

"He's being questioned by the police right now," Doc informed her, keeping the details vague.

As Doc hung up after securing the studio for later that evening, his mind busy with plans to investigate the attic and possibly find clues to clear Beano. He started the car, and Digger, sitting in the front passenger seat, suggested, "I reckon we ought to speak to the lead singer of Carnage, Skull Duggery."

"Why?" Jax asked from the back seat.

"I dunno, just thought maybe he might have some clues … we've got the time," Digger mused.

Doc nodded, his hands firm on the steering wheel as he merged the car into traffic. "We'll head to NewsLine … I'll ring around to get his number from there."

While Doc was busy making calls, Digger was chatting with Tilly, and Jax was talking to Janet.

"I can't believe all that's happened since the preview last night," Janet said, clearly shocked.

"We're thinking it might make a good Next File, what do you think?" Jax asked, hopeful for some guidance.

Janet chewed on the end of her pen, swivelling in her chair as she thought it over. After a moment, she answered, "We're not a true crime show, but in saying that, let's see how it develops. You've obviously got a gut feeling about it, Jax, and you do have a nose for a good story."

When Jax returned to Doc and Digger in the Next Files office, Doc was just finishing up a call. "I just spoke to Skull, he'll meet us at his rehearsal room at 6 pm."

"Good, where is it?" Jax asked.

"An abandoned warehouse in Petersham, not far from here. Oh, and I spoke to D.I. Malone, forensics found it wasn't blood on Beano's jacket, it was red paint. They're letting him go. I'll pick him up and take him home."

"Why don't you take him to lunch, he could do with a meal ... Then meet us back here to go see Skull," Jax suggested.

The afternoon passed quickly for Jax and Digger as they busied themselves writing up the post-production script for the last case, Bunyip. When Doc walked in, they realised just how quick the day had slipped by.

"Holy mackerel, is that the time?" Digger exclaimed.

Jax swivelled her chair around from her computer to face them. "All good with Beano?"

"Yep, took him to Maccas for lunch, not my choice, his, then dropped him off home. He said they gave him a heavy grilling at the cop-shop. Malone is convinced now there's a maniac on the loose."

"Has Beano remembered anything more?" Digger asked.

"Yes," Doc said, sitting on the edge of Digger's desk. "He remembered something that might have significance. He showed me the note Skull had emailed with the files, it said, 'There are the two files marked '1' and '2,' file 1 goes over the intro, file 2 goes over the middle 8, I want them backwards. Whatever you do DON'T play them together, they're separate for a reason. Skull.'"

"What's that supposed to mean, sounds like muso talk to me," Jax said.

Digger turned to her to explain, "The intro is the very beginning of the song, so Skull wanted file 1 played there and then the middle section of the song where there's like an instrumental break, he wanted file 2 played there."

"Oh, I get it. What was so special about the two files? And why backwards?" Jax asked.

"Though Skull recorded his voice, he couldn't properly flip them backwards ... so he wanted Beano to do that. Beano said forwards they sounded like Skull speaking in a foreign language, like Latin."

"So, let me get this straight," Jax thought out loud. "Beano gets the two tracks that are forwards but in a foreign language and reverses them so that they play back, backwards? Why?"

"To make it sound more demonic or something ... what I don't get is why he warned Beano not to play them together," Doc elaborated.

"Did he?" Digger asked. "Play them together?"

"He doesn't remember but thinks he might've ignored Skull's quirky warning, he's known for pranks."

"As his name suggests," Jax said. "We need to find out more about this."

"Has Beano still got the files he compiled?" Digger asked.

"No, they'd be at Atomic," Doc said, but he had something else on his mind. "Look, I thought it over driving back here, I don't think going and talking to Skull is right, it's Malone's job. I really don't think this a Next Files case, it's a murder investigation."

"I don't know Doc, I've got a gut feeling ... I don't think it's a typical murder scenario, I think there's more to it than meets the eye," Jax argued.

"I agree with Jax, I get the same feeling," Digger said.

"Well that's where we disagree, after talking with Beano, I see this as a straight up and down murder, some nutcase came into the studio that night, immediately after Beano left, found the guard and killed him. He then hid in the loft when Digger arrived and bolted after the cops had gone."

"Well, there are a few holes in your hypothesis, Doc," Jax said. "First, why did Beano leave everything on and has no memory of it? Secondly, how would the murderer know about the loft? Then, the big one, motive ... what's the motive?"

"You guys and your gut feelings ... I don't have any answers for you, Beano is still in the dark ... Alright, alright I'll go along with you but promise me the moment it starts getting hairy, like I mean, more a police matter, then we pull the plug. Agreed?"

Digger and Jax might've nodded in agreement, but they hadn't convinced Doc.

# CHAPTER
# FOUR

It was dark by the time they reached the turn into the narrow descending driveway to the old warehouse complex in Petersham. With only one light at the front of the long, single-story, hundred-metre-long building, Doc had to rely on the car headlights to navigate.

At the rear of the building, Doc spotted a parked van adorned with a skull decal and the words 'Carnage Asylum' emblazoned over it in script like a tattoo. He knew they were in the right place. A generator hummed in the rear of the van, feeding power along a cable into the building. They had only just gotten out of the car when the band cranked up the volume so loud it felt like all hell had broken loose.

Covering her ears, Jax yelled to Doc, "I'm not going in there, it'll give me brain damage."

"I'll go get him," Doc yelled back, determined.

Digger followed Doc, while Jax stayed inside the car.

A few minutes later, the music stopped, and Doc and Digger returned with Skull. Jax got out to greet him.

"Too loud for you, missy?" Skull said with a sinister snigger.

Jax had never seen anyone quite like Skull before; his menacing appearance sent a shiver up her spine.

"Doc filled me in on what happened at Atomic. Unreal. What can I say, I told Beano not to mess with the incantation," Skull said in a gruff voice.

"Incantation?" Jax repeated, intrigued.

"Yeah, I warned him. Those words when put together can summon a demon … and I'd say that's what happened."

"Wait a minute … it was sorcery, occultism?" Doc queried.

"Sure was … what do you expect for a song called Hellhouse?" he said, amused.

"Where did you get a conjuring hex like that? I mean, one that's for real," Jax asked, sceptical yet curious.

"What do you mean 'for real'? Don't you believe in the occult, missy?" Skull growled.

"I believe in the spirit world, but I'm not sure about conjuring demons," Jax admitted.

"It's from the Book of Shadows, a Wiccan book. No-one knows how old it is," Skull explained.

Digger chimed in, "So you just looked up how to conjure a demon, recorded the spell, broke it into two parts, and sent it to Beano to put on the track backwards?"

"Yeah, something like that."

Doc, Digger, and Jax were lost for words, the situation too bizarre to fully grasp.

"So we're dealing with witchcraft here," Doc summed up.

"Yeah, I suppose you are."

"You don't seem too worried that your spell might have conjured a demon that killed a man," Jax said angrily.

"Hey, I warned Beano … it wasn't meant to do any harm."

"So how can you undo it? The spell…" Jax pressed.

Skull thought about it, but before he could answer, one of the band members stepped out of the darkness and yelled, "You coming back to rehearse, Skull, or you gonna talk all freakin' night?"

"I've gotta get back … I honestly don't know how to reverse it … if you can. Maybe you can research it … The Book of Shadows. Sorry, Doc, that's all I can tell ya." He walked off back to rehearsal, leaving the others dumbfounded.

In the car on the way to Atomic Studio, the atmosphere was charged with tension and disbelief. Jax was the first to break the silence. "It looks like it's something a bit more than a madman on the loose."

"You can't take what Skull said as gospel, Jax, he's pretty twisted," Doc cautioned, keeping his eyes on the road.

Digger had been quiet, absorbed in his thoughts. Jax turned to him, "What do you think, Digger?"

"I reckon it'll happen again if those tapes aren't erased, quick smart," Digger finally said, his voice grave.

"I agree," Doc replied resolutely, surprising Jax a bit.

"So, then you think there is something to what Skull said then?" Jax probed, knowing Doc was usually more conservative in his beliefs.

"A precaution, that's all," Doc answered, his tone suggesting he was hedging his bets.

"Right," Jax said, sensing that Doc was indeed taking an each-way-bet approach. "I need to get hold of that Book of Shadows."

Digger, ever resourceful, began searching on his phone. "I just asked AI, and it said, 'The most famous Book of Shadows was created by the pioneering Wiccan Gerald Gardner sometime in the late 1940s. It has been used in serious covens ever since. It contains religious text and magical spells...'"

"I remember the Book of Shadows from the TV show 'Charmed' in the late '90s," Doc chimed in, a slight smile playing on his lips.

"Ha! Didn't think you of all people would've watched Charmed," Jax scoffed, amused.

"It goes on," Digger interrupted, focusing back on his phone. "The Book of Shadows is a grimoire; a witches' textbook of magic ... it was originally titled 'Ye Book of Ye Art Magical'. An updated version was devised by the occultist Aleister Crowley. Later Doreen Valiente became high priestess of the famed Bricket Wood coven in England, and produced yet another version of The Book of Shadows omitting Crowley's update. The original Crowley version is said to contain conjuring rituals that can only be found in covens and is sometimes called 'The Book of Mirrors', 'The Tree', 'The Book of Ways' or simply 'The Book'. The Book of Shadows was mentioned in the trailer of 'Blair Witch 2', but was not in the film. In the Australian television series 'Nowhere Boys' two characters are known to possess a Book of Shadows. It also appeared in the role-playing game 'Dungeons and Dragons,' enabling warlock class to learn extra spells and rituals."

"Okay, ask it where we can get a copy of the Crowley version," Jax instructed.

"It said it's only obtainable through a coven," Digger relayed the information.

"So you might have to become a witch to get hold of a copy, Jax," Doc joked with a sarcastic laugh.

"Now there's a challenge," Jax countered.

"Why not ask Skull for a loan of his copy," Digger suggested.

Doc parked a short walk from Atomic Studios and called Skull, who surprisingly answered his phone. "Skull, rehearsals finished? Oh, okay, listen, do you have a copy of The Book of Shadows? No, so how did you get hold of the ... oh, alright, can you text it to me? Good, thanks man. We just arrived at Atomic. Yes, we plan to erase the tape." He hung up as they reached the studio entrance, pausing to update Jax and Digger. "He doesn't have a copy of the book," Doc announced as his phone buzzed with a text. "He just sent the contact of his friend, or a fan, Vanessa her name is; she gave him the incantation."

"Is she in a coven?" Jax asked.

"Yes, she's a high priestess, lives in Balmain. I'll give her a call once we've finished up here."

As they entered the building, a muffled scream echoed from the end of the corridor. "Was that a scream?" Doc asked, quickening his pace toward the noise.

They rushed through the door of the studio, where they found Cindy standing at the console, visibly shaken. Doc signalled for Jax and Digger to wait by the door while he approached Cindy cautiously. "Cindy, it's Doc Lee ... what happened?"

Cindy, sobbing, her red-rimmed glasses matching her short red hair, pointed tremblingly at the studio window. "It was there, a monster, looking back at me!"

Doc glanced at the window, seeing only their reflections. "It's okay Cindy, calm down, you're safe, sit down ... tell me about it."

Cindy took a couple of deep breaths, trying to compose herself, and sat down. Doc turned her chair away from the window to face him and the others. "These are my associates, Jax and Digger de Loite. They were here with the police yesterday, so they know what happened to the guard and Beano. Now, tell us what happened to you."

"After I finished the class, the kids left, and I set up Beano's Hellhouse tape for you guys ... Then Beano called; he asked me to send him the files of the mix so he could finish it on Pro Tools at home," Cindy explained.

"Right, Pro Tools is a mixing app," Doc clarified for Jax and Digger.

"I set up the tape and then sent the stems to Beano by WeTransfer," Cindy continued.

"Okay, then what happened?" Doc prompted.

"I hadn't played it ... but I noticed after I sent it off that there was a separate section on the timeline after the track. I wondered what it was and played it. It was weird, someone, I guess it was Skull, talking in a foreign language that had been flipped."

"So it was backwards?" Doc confirmed.

"Yes, you can easily tell even if it's in a strange language," Cindy said then continued. "Suddenly the room got cold, like the aircon had been turned up ... the ceiling lights flickered ... and when I looked at the window..." She paused on the edge of panic.

"It's okay, it's okay..." Doc reassured her.

"Um, there was a monster staring back at me from the window," Cindy finished.

Jax asked, "Was it on the other side in the studio or a reflection?"

Cindy looked intently at Jax, then replied anxiously, "It was my reflection, and it was terrible. Big yellow goat's eyes, pointed teeth, a ghoul ... but while it was my reflection, it seemed to have a life of its own. I screamed, and then you came in."

Jax felt a chill, and Digger scanned the room, uneasy about the possibility of the monster still lurking. Doc was deep in thought. Jax had an epiphany, locked eyes with Cindy, and asked worriedly, "You didn't send the second part on the timeline to Beano, did you?"

Cindy thought for a moment then admitted, "Yes, I did."

Jax looked sharply at Doc and said grimly, "Oh, shit!"

# CHAPTER FIVE

On the way to Beano's house, Jax explained, "I think the incantation conjures up a demon that possesses whoever is present. When Beano played it, he got possessed ... and when Cindy played it—"

"Wait, Beano bolted from the studio just minutes before the guard showed up. The demon, or whoever, had to be inside—that couldn't have been Beano," Doc argued while driving.

Digger piped up with a thought, "What if the thing in the window really does have a life of its own, like Cindy said? What if it's not just a reflection, but an actual demon?"

"Then why didn't it attack us when it was Cindy's reflection?"

"Maybe 'cause Cindy was still there," Digger guessed.

"I think you're onto something, Digger. Like, once this thing is called up, it takes over the host, then ditches the host to do its dirty work. That's why Beano didn't remember a thing about the guard."

"Yeah, and we rocked up just in time with Cindy and smashed the spell," Digger added.

Things were starting to click for them.

Jax threw in her two cents, "Maybe it only sticks around for a bit; after it dealt with the guard, it zipped back to wherever it came from—another dimension or something."

"I don't know, that's all a bit too out-there for me," Doc said.

"Okay, so what's your take?" Jax challenged.

"I reckon the incantation messes with your head, kinda like a drug ... could spark a violent snap, memory loss..."

"Then how do you explain Beano ducking out before what went down with the guard?" Digger challenged.

"The incantation kept playing … Beano left it on, so the guard got the full blast … it might've made him totally lose it," Doc explained.

"Well, either way, we gotta catch up with Beano before he plays that track and sets off something seriously ugly."

Bindi and her two schoolmates, Tiddles and Sheila, were crossing the small bridge over Tarban Creek at the end of Gladesville Road. They'd been to Maccas in Gladesville, and it would be another ten minutes before they reached Beano's house further along the narrow, tree-lined road. Eating fries, they were giggling, ribbing each other about their crushes at school.

The spare room on the second floor of Beano's house was professionally set up for recording and mixing, virtually a replica of the control room at Atomic without a console, an effects rack, and large recorders. Instead, it boasted a pair of Genelec 8351B SAM speakers positioned on stands on either side of a desk. The desk held a top-of-the-range 24-inch M3 iMac and a second 27-inch Apple Studio HD display. With the light from the screens reflecting off his glasses and his long, unruly curly hair, Beano sat in a swivel chair, reorganising the timeline of Hellouse on ProTools. He leaned back, content with all the stems he'd dragged onto the timeline from the WeTransfer folder Cindy had sent him—it was time to play the new mix he'd previously assembled at Atomic. Everything was in place except for the controversial new section Skull had recorded, which appeared as a single file on the timeline after the end of the song. To complete the track to Skull's specification, he would still need to copy the voices to the opening and the middle eight. He'd get around to doing that later; for now, he wanted to trim the track, making small changes to improve the balance. He hit play.

Doc was getting frustrated at the traffic jam they were in. "At this rate, it'll take another forty minutes to get to Beano's!"

His phone rang, it was on hands-free speaker. "Hello, who's this?"

"My name's Vanessa, Skull asked me to call you."

"Oh, hi Vanessa," he gave Digger beside him a raised eyebrow glance. "I'm in a car on speaker with my two associates, Jax and Digger ... we have a few questions for you about the incantation you gave Skull for his song Hellhouse."

"Yup, go ahead then," Vanessa's voice was husky and sexy.

Jax spoke up, "Hey Vanessa, it's Jax. I'll cut to the chase. That incantation, when played according to the instructions, summoned something evil. Do you get that?"

"Yes, that's very possible. I told Skull to be very careful how he used it. I gave him specific inst..."

Jax cut her off, "It wasn't his fault, it was Beano, the producer-engineer mixing the recording ... Skull passed on your instructions, but Beano ignored them."

"I see."

"So we assume it came from the Book of Shadows?"

"Yes."

"The original Crowley version?"

"Yes, the only one in Australia, I believe. I inherited it."

"So you have it?"

"Yes. What do you need to know?"

"What can be conjured by it?" Jax asked emphatically.

"Well, because of the song title and the context of the lyrics, I gave him an evocation of the 12 Kings of Hell, specifically Choronzon. Look, I can't tell you much more than that."

"Hey Vanessa, a guy was murdered because of the evocation you gave Skull. Do you want the police to know that?"

"That's not my fault. The summoning is readily available to anyone who wants to take the time to find it."

"But it wasn't just some random anyone, it was you, Vanessa. Now, help me here," Jax appealed aggressively.

There was silence while Vanessa mulled it over. She then said, "Alright, what else do you want to know?"

"How does it take its prey? ... where does it go once it has fed, and how do you get rid of it?" Jax asked.

"Okay, okay, if evoked, it takes the form of its host. It then feeds by taking a soul..."

"How?" Digger asked.

"Through the eyes of the victim."

"Then where does it go?"

"Once its hunger is sated, it returns to whence it came."

"Another dimension?" Jax queried.

"Yes, if you like ... How do you get rid of Choronzon? ... Well, you don't. Once the demon has taken a soul, it will return to hell. While that recording exists, Choronzon will be a threat."

"Thank you, Vanessa," Doc said.

They fell silent, thinking, then Digger said, "From what she explained, Beano is safe if he's alone when he plays it."

"What about his cousin, Bindi?" Doc said worriedly.

Bindi and her friends reached Beano's house and stopped at the front gate.

"Hey Bindi, is, like, your joint haunted or something ... it looks it?" Sheila said, the sassy one of the three.

"Yep, by my cousin, Beano," she joked.

"Heard he's a record producer," Tiddles said.

"Isn't he doing Carnage Asylum's new single?" Sheila said, in the know. "Skull Duggery is to die for."

Knowing they were busting to look inside the house, Bindi asked coyly, "So do you guys wanna come in?"

Sheila and Tiddles nodded animatedly, so Bindi led them through the rusted old front gate and into the house.

Inside, Sheila looked around and said with a giggle, "This is like the Addams Family, where's Thing?"

Tiddles giggled, but Bindi wasn't so amused. Hellhouse suddenly blared from upstairs, and Sheila reacted.

"Alright, that's Carnage Asylum, I can tell it anywhere ... serious! Can we go up and listen ... can we, can we?"

"No, not while Beano's working; he gets pissed if I interrupt him."

"Aw, I'd just stand outside the door to listen," Sheila insisted.

"Okay, okay, but don't make any noise."

"You coming, Tiddles?"

"No way … it looks too spooky."

Sheila pulled a scrunched-up face at Tiddles and then started up the staircase.

Happy with how it was sounding, Beano was making minor adjustments to the track on the fly. The song finished, and he hit the space bar to stop the cursor. He needed to adjust the fade-out. As he was doing that, he heard a click behind him and swivelled around to find Sheila standing in the doorway. A pretty blonde in a school uniform was the last thing he expected to see.

"Sorry to disturb you, but I'm a big fan of Carnage Asylum. Any chance I can hear it from the top?"

"And who are you?"

"Sheila … Bindi's friend."

"Didn't Bindi tell you I don't like to be disturbed while I'm working?"

She shot him a bewitching look, "She did, but you know … I thought you might make an exception … I'd be really grateful."

She got the better of him. "Okay, come in, close the door, and you can hear it once and once only."

She did as he instructed and then ambled over to him shy schoolgirl-like.

"Can I sit on your knee to listen," she said flirtatiously.

Beano fell for it, knowing it was wrong but unable to resist. She sat on his knee ready to hear it.

Beano hit play. But distracted and not thinking clearly, the track played from where he'd finished, after the fade-out. A demonic voice in a weird language rumbled through the speakers, backwards.

In the living room, Bindi, noticing the music had stopped, went over to the staircase and looked up. Sheila wasn't there. "Sheila?" she called out.

Tiddles joined her, fiddling with one of her two long brown plaits asked, "Do you think went into the studio room?"

"Oh no!" Bindi exclaimed and started up the stairs in a hurry. Tiddles wasn't going to be left alone in the spooky house and raced up after her.

Doc pulled the car up outside Beano's house, and they got out. He led the way up to the front door and knocked, when there was no answer he tested the door handle—it was open. They entered. Inside Doc said, "I don't know where his studio is upstairs or downstairs…"

Jax cut him off, "Shush, listen…"

The three of them listened. They could hear a deep voice speaking in an unfamiliar tongue. "That's it!" Digger said, "That's the spell. It's coming from upstairs."

Digger quickly led the three of them up the stairs. The corridor was deserted—they stopped and listened for the voice—it was coming from a room three doors along. Digger pointed at it. The voice was now in the second part of the evocation. Before they could move, a loud girl's scream erupted from the room, and Beano emerged right through the door, stopping dead in his tracks in front of them. It looked vaguely like Beano; dressed like him, but his face was grotesque, demonic. They knew immediately what had happened.

"Don't look him in the eye!" Jax exclaimed. "It's Choronzon!"

# CHAPTER SIX

Avoiding eye contact with the demon, Jax noticed an oval antique-looking mirror mounted on the wall. She yanked it off and, holding it up like a shield with the reflective surface facing Choronzon, she edged toward the demon with Digger and Doc huddled behind her. A rattle at the door signalled it was about to be opened; Jax yelled out, "Stay where you are, don't come out!"

Choronzon backed up along the corridor showing distress—the mirror was obviously working. Jax bravely took a peek around the mirror just in time to see Choronzon rush at the window at the end of the corridor and vanish right through it. "It's gone," she said with relief, lowering the mirror.

"Where?" Doc questioned.

"It just, like, dissolved through the window," Jax put down the mirror.

"Guess it didn't like its own reflection. What made you think that'd work, sis?" Digger asked.

"The 8 Dragons case, the ghost feared its own reflection. Worth a try."

"Glad you did."

Doc had walked to the window and was looking out. "Can't see it anywhere. Where would it go? Has it fed?"

Jax opened the door and stepped inside the studio. The three girls were huddled together, Beano sprawled out on the floor. Jax went over to the girls and asked, "You guys okay, anyone hurt?"

Bindi spoke up with a trembling voice, "No, what was that thing?"

Digger brought Beano around and then helped him up into the chair asking, "Beano, Beano, you with us?"

Beano looked at Digger vaguely and mumbled, "Yeah, what happened?"

"You were playing Hellhouse, remember?"

"No, last thing I remember was coming home."

"His memory is blank," Digger reported as Doc entered.

"Everyone okay? Beano?" Doc said, surprised, not expecting him to be there. "But I thought...?"

Jax had a theory. "Choronzon must've possessed him but then for some reason left him in his image."

"It was when the voice was played again," Sheila said.

"Tell us exactly what happened, um?" Jax asked.

"Sheila, that's me, this is Bindi and Tiddles..."

"Yes, we know Bindi. Go on," Jax asked.

"I'm a Carnage Asylum fan, so Beano was playing me Hellhouse, Bindi and Tiddles came in to listen as well. Instead of the song playing another part started; a demonic voice speaking in a weird language. I looked at that computer screen, the one turned off and saw a reflection of Beano's face ... it was like morphing, changing, freaky. I jumped up..."

"Where were you sitting?"

She looked all guilty and said, "On Beano's knee."

Jax raised an eyebrow and said sternly, "Hmm, go on."

"Beano was like glued to the screen ... it was only his reflection that was the creepy thing, he was still normal but like all frozen. I tried to stop the voice playing and pressed the keyboard, it didn't work, it just started playing it over again. I pressed it again and it turned on the screen with the monster in it. Doing that must've forced it out of the screen, like it dragged itself out ... but it was like freaking out because when I'd hit the keyboard to stop it the first time it sped the voice up. The thing was holding its ears totally freaking  out ... Tiggles screamed, and it raced at the door and went right through it like a ghost. I pulled the power on the computer, shutting it down."

"That all makes sense," Jax said.

"What was it?" Bindi asked, her voice still shaky.

"A demon, conjured up by that creepy voice on the track," Digger explained.

"How can that even happen?" Tiddles asked, her voice a whimper.

"Skull Duggery used some ancient words, like a spell, that summoned the demon, Choronzon, when played backwards."

"What did it want?" Sheila chimed in.

Jax glanced at Doc, not sure what to say and not wanting to freak out the girls any more than they already were.

Doc took over. "It wanted to take over whoever summoned it."

"So, that was Beano?" Sheila probed.

"Yes," Doc confirmed.

"Where is it now?" Tiddles pressed nervously.

"It went out through the hallway window. I checked but couldn't see it anywhere," Doc reported.

Tiddles looked ready to freak out. Bindi caught that, pulled her in for a hug, and asked, "Is it coming back? Is it out there? Are we safe?"

"We don't know, love," Doc admitted softly.

Three schoolboys had just wrapped up rugby practice at St Joseph's College football field and were taking the shortcut to Gladesville Road. The path cut through a small thicket of trees and bushes leading to the bus stop on Gladesville Road. The wind was picking up; trees swayed ominously against the dark sky, urging the boys to speed up with rain on the horizon.

It was their usual path home after practice, and they'd braved sketchy weather before, but tonight had a weird, spooky vibe they couldn't shake.

All in the same year 12 class, Phil was the leader. As the rugby team captain and big for his age, he was usually fearless. He led them down the narrow path, branches whipping around in the wind like creepy fingers trying to grab them. With the storm brewing, Phil's usually brave buddies were losing their cool. Lightning flashed, thunder boomed, and they freaked. Phil picked up the pace just as the skies opened up. Up ahead, despite the torrential downpour,

Phil spotted car lights on Gladesville Road next to the bus shelter. They bolted for it, skidding into the shelter breathless and soaked but relieved to be out of the storm. They laughed off their scare, glad to be dry. A bus approached, headlights blurry with rain. Phil checked it out, "Not ours," he said, then glanced at a girl sitting quietly by herself, wondering if she was waiting for this one, maybe dozing off.

"Miss," Phil said, trying to be polite, "are you waiting for the bus to Pittwater Road?"

As the bus slowed, its headlights illuminated the shelter lighting it up inside—suddenly, they could see her clearly. Her face was a horror show, dark bloody pits where her eyes should have been, blood-streaked cheeks—she was dead—Choronzon had fed.

✗

In the living room, Doc told Jax and Digger, "I'll drive Sheila and Tiddles home."

Bindi pleaded, "Please don't leave us alone."

Jax wrapped her in a hug, "It's okay love, we'll stay here, right Digger?"

Digger, glancing up from his phone, nodded, "Yep, sure will."

Beano, slumped on the couch with his face in his hands, still struggling to grasp what had happened to him, twice, looked up and said, "Can I tag along for the ride? I need some fresh air."

Doc nodded, "Cool, let's go."

With Sheila and Tiddles in the back seat and Beano riding shotgun, Doc pulled out onto Gladesville Road. They hadn't gone far when they encountered strobing police and ambulance lights and an officer directing traffic in the middle of the road.

"Must be a car accident," Doc muttered.

As they passed the bus shelter on the other side, it became clear it was a crime scene, not a car wreck. Three boys stood off to the side, talking to a detective.

Beano exclaimed, "Hey, that's DI Malone."

Doc quickly pulled over, and an officer immediately rushed over and tapped on his window. Doc rolled it down.

"You'll need to move on, sir," the officer instructed.

"We need to speak with DI Malone over there, urgently," Doc stated. The cop nodded and then stepped away.

"Girls, stay put," Beano instructed as he and Doc exited the car and headed towards the crime scene.

"Wonder what's going on?" Tiddles murmured.

"Guess what?" Sheila said, sporting a devious grin.

"What?"

Sheila held up a thumb drive. "I copied it."

"What?"

"Hellhouse. I downloaded it from Beano's computer when no-one was looking," she confessed with a snigger.

"How random! You'll be the first at school with a copy of Carnage Asylum's new single."

"Yep, I can post it on socials and get thousands of hits."

"Better keep it quiet, do it under a fake name."

"I will," Sheila agreed conspiratorially.

As they approached the cluster of police, Beano asked Doc, "Did you meet Malone?"

"No."

"Better let me do the introductions then, he's a tough cookie."

Malone had just finished talking to Phil and the boys when he noticed Beano coming over.

"What the hell are you doing here?" Malone questioned.

"I live up the road. This is Doc Lee, he works with Jax on The Next…"

"Yeah, I know, I've seen him on the show. What is it with you guys, your show following me? Here we are, same MO as Atomic," Malone said condemningly.

The police cleared a path for paramedics to wheel a gurney through, giving Doc and Beano a clear view of the victim. On the bench inside the shelter sat a girl, probably in her late teens, staring in their direction, her eyes just hollow voids.

"Oh, no," Doc murmured, glancing at Beano, who was stunned—they both knew what had happened.

# CHAPTER
# SEVEN

"**S**o let me get this straight," Malone said sceptically. "You pair of fruit-loops are saying whoever killed the guard at Atomic Studios also killed that young woman over there?"

"Yes, you need to understand how it happens," Beano pleaded. "Come to my place and I'll show you, it's only up the road."

The detective looked at Beano as if he were insane, then turned to Doc, "You think I can be convinced?"

"That's up to you, detective. We can only show you what we've found."

"All right, give me fifteen minutes and I'll go with you, but you better not be wasting my time."

"We'll just drop a couple of people home and be back in fifteen," Doc said.

✗

Beano led DI Malone and Doc into his house where they found Jax, Bindi, and Digger sitting in the living room watching TV.

"So, the whole gang's here," Malone remarked derisively.

Beano said, "Follow me, detective."

Malone obliged and followed Beano up to the studio. Doc stayed behind to fill the others in on what had happened and why they'd run into DI Malone.

Beano showed Malone the timeline on his computer and explained, without playing it, how the demon had been conjured. The others entered and listened to Beano's explanation.

When Beano finished, Malone turned to Jax and said, "Sounds like one of your Next Files."

"You're right about that, and what Beano explained is exactly what happened," Jax affirmed confidently.

Malone said, "You understand how difficult that is to believe, don't you? Can you imagine how a judge would react to me explaining how two people had their souls sucked out through their eyes by a demon conjured up by a heavy metal song?"

"It isn't easy to accept, but things supernatural never are," Jax replied.

Beano swivelled around in his chair with a worried look on his face, "I hate to be the bearer of more bad news, but someone's downloaded the song which includes the incantation."

"What?" Jax almost screamed. "How do you know?"

"The computer lists the downloads, see."

Jax took a look. It clearly showed there had been a download. "Who would have downloaded it?"

"Sheila," Bindi interjected. "That's the sort of thing she'd do. She had a thumb drive."

"We've gotta get that thing before she summons Choronzon again," Digger said urgently.

"Choronzon? What, this thing's got a name?" Malone questioned.

"Google it, detective … see what we're up against," Jax suggested grimly.

Sitting on the couch and surfing messages on his phone, Detective Malone wasn't sure what to believe. In his twenty years as a detective, he'd never come across anything like this. As sceptical as he was, he had no choice but to follow the lead of the teenagers. Much as he disliked doing so, he couldn't help being impressed by their knowledge and investigative skills. He thought to himself, 'It's no wonder The Next Files is a hit.'

He'd searched Choronzon on the net and was amazed by the details. While Bindi was trying to get hold of Sheila, and Jax, Beano, and Doc were discussing tactics, Digger sat next to Malone.

"Hard to believe, isn't it?" Digger said.

Malone looked up from his phone. "I've just read about this Choronzon ... all this demon stuff is another world from the one we live in ... I thought it was just the stuff of movies and novels."

"I've only been with The Next Files team a short time. Part of my job is reading through all the thousands of supernatural and unexplainable witness accounts ... that's how The Next Files came about. So many had been accumulated at NewsLine, never investigated, so they gave them to an intern, my sister, Jax. They'd never expected her to solve some of them."

"Why did they have all the accounts in the first place?"

"The TV channel had 'The X-Files' in the 90s, remember that show?"

"Yeah, Fox Mulder and Scully, who could forget it."

"Well, a lot of people were so touched by the show that they sent their personal experiences to NewsLine. I tell you, there are boxes of 'em. So, we wade through them looking for reports that seem legit and then investigate them."

"I get it, that's how you got the 8 Dragons and the Min Min lights stories."

"Yep, the most recent two that aired were pretty wild, one about a witch in Malaysia and the one when I came on board in, Blood of Aztecs ... that was us looking for our father in the jungles of Mindanao."

"Was all that for real?"

"Absolutely ... even more than we could ever cram into 48 minutes of television. We just finished a new story about a bunyip out near Leeton."

"So, how did you come across this demon thing then?"

"By accident. In his free time, Doc plays in a band called The Time Benders, their live mixing engineer is Beano. I was chatting to him after a gig and he told me he was going to Atomic to mix the new single for Carnage Asylum and if I liked, I could drop in. That led to all this."

Doc came over. "Bindi spoke to Sheila's mother, said she went out not long after we dropped her home. She doesn't know where she is."

"Can Bindi take a guess?"

"Yes, she said it's Friday night and there's a sleepover going on at one of their friends. She rang the friends but Sheila wasn't there yet."

"Has she got a cell phone I can track?" Malone said, getting up ready for action.

Doc turned and called out, "Bindi, what's Sheila's number?"

There was no need for Beano or Bindi to join, so Jax, Digger, and Doc accompanied Malone in his unmarked police vehicle. Malone had tracked Sheila's phone to an abandoned building at the rear of the long-disused Tarban Creek Lunatic Asylum. Along the way, Jax read out a search on the place.

"Opened in 1838 and closed in 1968, Tarban Creek Lunatic Asylum was the forerunner to the more widely known Gladesville Mental Hospital, which operated from 1868 to 1993. Says here there's not much left of it."

"Kids your age hold rave parties at places like this, and other frightening spots like Waverly Cemetery. That's about as weird as it gets for us cops," Malone said with a snigger.

Another storm was brewing; rolling clouds were lighting up purple from intermittent lightning flashes to the south.

"It's going to come down huge in less than an hour," Digger noted, peering out the window.

Malone activated the indicator and turned into a narrow driveway, eyes on the tracking app on his dash-mounted phone.

The derelict Asylum building was an old, single-storey structure, roughly the size of an average bungalow in serious disrepair. Yet, it retained a touch of grandeur with two classic convict-cut sandstone pillars flanking the front entrance, reminiscent of an ancient Greek temple. Surrounded by a tall wire fence, signs posted by the NSW Government Heritage Department sternly warned, 'Do not enter'. Despite its rundown appearance, the air buzzed with the intense vibrations of death metal music. Through windows left bare of glass, the interior was lit by candles, casting flickering shadows on the walls of people dancing. The powerful distorted guitars and the wicked, growling vocals of Skull Duggery were shaking the structure.

Inside, about thirty people were dancing, most lost in the throbbing pulse of the music. The DJ, his face obscured by an extreme mop of hair, was headbanging to the Carnage Asylum track 'Possession' that blared from the speakers. At the end of the room, overlooking the dance floor, four director's chairs were arranged in a row. Seated in the central chair, which seemed larger than the others, was Skull Duggery. His presence dominated the space, amplified by his stature and the intensity with which he surveyed the room. Flanked by girls sporting gothic attire, one of them was Sheila. She leaned towards him, raising her voice to be heard over the music, "Skull, let me send you a song, you're gonna love it."

She transferred it from her phone to his. He popped in his earbuds and cracked a smile when he recognised it was Beano's latest mix of 'Hellhouse.' What they didn't know was that when the track ended the incantation would play.

Skull shot Sheila a wicked grin, bobbing his head to the beat, totally psyched she had snagged it for him.

Malone turned on his high-beam to light up a dark tunnel that was part of the entrance. The headlights revealed eerie graffiti splashed across the walls of the dome-roofed passage, stretching about thirty-metres.

"Judging by the graffiti, this place is a magnet for the lunatic fringe," Digger remarked.

As they came out of the tunnel, they saw a bunch of cars, a van, and four Harley choppers parked outside a wire perimeter fence. Malone pulled up next to them. Through the fence, they could see the flickering candlelight from inside the building and, with the engine off, hear the pulsing beat of metal.

"There you go, an underground rave," Malone said. "Totally illegal, especially here since it's part of a historical site … but that's not what brought us."

While grooving to 'Hellhouse,' Skull stood up and headed to the back of the room to better hear the track through his earbuds. As the song neared its end, he found himself checking his reflection in a glass pane of a door—the only sheet of glass that hadn't been shattered in the whole place. Just then, the incantation began to play. It was a new twist—he hadn't heard it played backwards before. Watching closely, his reflection began to morph: his eyes first turned into glowing yellow goat's eyes, then his teeth started to elongate and sharpen. Intrigued, he grinned to get a clearer view of the eerie transformation. Suddenly, he realised what was happening, but it was already too late. He collapsed to the floor as the demonic image of Choronzon sneered mockingly down at him from the glass pane in the door.

# CHAPTER EIGHT

Sheila was waiting for Skull when she spotted him heading towards a side exit. She quickly got up to follow, curious about his thoughts on the song.

Malone led the group through a man-sized hole in the wire fence, pausing on the other side to give instructions. "Doc, take the back. Jax, you're on the right side. And Digger, you're with me. Cellphones," he added, prompting them to pull out their phones. "Add this," he read out his number, "and call if you spot anything. Don't engage with anyone or anything threatening, got it?" They all nodded in agreement.

Inside, the DJ was cross-fading 'Possession' with another Carnage Asylum track, 'Blade of Slaughter.' Malone and Digger entered unnoticed, scanning the crowd.

"They're all off their faces," Digger noted, loud enough to rise above the music. "Can't see Sheila anywhere."

Malone, looking out of place in his wrinkled grey suit and tie, moved through the dancefloor to the back. Just as Digger caught up, Malone noticed someone face down on the floor. Kneeling down, he rolled the unconscious person over.

"That's Skull Duggery," Digger announced, kneeling beside him and removing one of Skull's earbuds to listen—Hellhouse was on loop. Showing the buds to Malone, he said, "Looks like he's heard the incantation."

Listening again as the song was about to end, Digger acted swiftly, searching Skull's jacket for his phone, hitting stop just in time. Relieved, he looked up at Malone. "That was close, it was just about to play the incantation," he explained, handing over the phone and earbuds.

At the back of the building, Doc found two guys passionately kissing against the wall by the rear door. Unfazed, he continued on. The area was dark and cluttered with debris, the ground overgrown with weeds. He had to move some boards leaning against the building to make his way. A flash of lightning briefly illuminated the rubbish on the ground, thunder followed, mismatched with the music's beat, and it began to drizzle. Doc glanced up, cursing the miserable outside task he'd been dealt.

Jax was edging along the side of the building when she passed a young couple under the eave lighting a joint. They looked at her as if she were an alien. Suddenly, she saw Sheila dash out of the building, seemingly chasing someone. "Sheila! Stop!" Jax shouted, but Sheila didn't respond and picked up her pace.

As the lightning intensified and the rain grew heavier, Sheila saw Skull up ahead. He had gone through the barrier fence and was heading towards the main road. She ran along the fence, stopping to grasp the wire and shouted, "Skull, where are you going, wait?" He stopped and in a low demonic voice said, "Come to me." Sheila rolled her eyes—this was exactly what she had hoped for ... Skull was her crush ... this was her chance. She noticed a gap in the fence just large enough for her, climbed through, and continued her pursuit as Skull reached the road and entered a tunnel.

Jax reached the fence out of breath and looked for a way through. Seeing Sheila running towards the road and the tunnel, she yelled, "Sheila! Stop! Wait!" But it was no use; Sheila had already slipped into the tunnel. Jax found the hole Sheila used, squeezed through, and ran towards the tunnel.

Inside the dark tunnel, Sheila slowed to a walk. Skull had stopped a few metres ahead, his back to her. Lightning illuminated the graffiti on the walls, thunder echoing inside the tunnel. She approached Skull, and asked, "Skull?"

He turned just as a lightning flash revealed his grotesque face. Sheila froze, realising this wasn't the Skull she knew.

Footsteps echoed as Jax ran into the tunnel, slowing as she saw the silhouettes ahead. "Sheila, it's Jax."

Another lightning flash illuminated the figure more clearly, and Sheila let out a scream louder than the thunder, echoing through the tunnel.

Jax realised the towering figure must be Choronzon.

Doc heard Sheila's scream and immediately took off towards the sound. The rain was pouring down harder now. As he ran, he phoned Malone. "It's Doc, I heard a scream from the tunnel we passed through ... I'm on my way there now."

Malone glanced towards the side exit and, with Digger in tow, dashed towards the tunnel.

Inside the tunnel, Jax spoke calmly and decisively to Sheila. "Don't panic, Sheila ... just turn slowly and walk towards me." But Sheila remained frozen, unresponsive to Jax. From five metres away, Jax could see Choronzon's eyes glowing yellow as he stared intently at Sheila, seemingly poised to draw her soul out through her eyes, and Jax knew it. Amidst the noise of the torrential rain, with lightning flashing and thunder booming, Jax felt helpless but knew she had to act. Without giving it a second thought, she sprinted towards Sheila and tackled her to the ground.

Sitting on the young girl's chest, Jax looked into her eyes, then up at Choronzon and yelled, "Be gone, Choronzon, go to hell!" She glanced back down at Sheila just as the sound of loud footsteps entered the tunnel.

Doc appeared first, closely followed by Digger and Malone. They skidded to a halt beside Jax, still straddling Sheila.

"What happened?" Doc panted, out of breath.

Jax looked up to find that Choronzon had vanished into thin air.

Turning to Doc, she replied, "Didn't you see Choronzon?"

"No, there was no-one on you two," Doc responded, clearly surprised. "Is Sheila alright?"

Jax helped Sheila to her feet. "Yes, her eyes are intact, but it was a close call, wasn't it, Sheila?"

Sheila looked around, dazed, and asked, "Where am I?"

The rain had passed, and the four of them escorted Sheila back towards Malone's car.

"I better go check on Skull," Digger mentioned along the way. "Give me the phone and his buds."

"You'd better erase that song," Malone stressed.

Digger immediately deleted it.

"Meet us at the car," Malone instructed Digger.

Digger returned through the fence and re-entered the building.

A new track, "Wings of Leather, Wings of Steel," was pulsing through the speakers. He spotted Skull sitting in his director's chair, commanding the room. Approaching him, Digger handed over the earbuds and phone, shouting over the music, "These yours?"

Skull patted his pockets, then looked at Digger quizzically. "Yeah, how come you've got them? Who are you anyway?"

"The gatekeeper of Hellhouse," Digger retorted sharply, then turned and walked away, leaving Skull with the impression he'd just had a paranormal encounter—a notion Digger knew was accurate.

Outside Sheila's house, Malone surveyed it through the windshield. "By the look of your home, you come from a wealthy family, Sheila. If I were you, I'd be more cautious about your choice of friends."

Stepping out of the car, her black goth makeup smeared by the rain, Sheila glanced back at Malone and remarked slyly, "You'll never be me, detective." She slammed the door with disdain.

"If she only knew how close she came," Jax murmured.

Malone then drove to Beano's house to drop them off.

Parked in front of the stark building, Digger shook Malone's hand. "How are you going to explain the two deaths?"

"Right now, I have no idea—take care, Digger."

Doc, already out of the car, reached in and shook Malone's hand as well. "Thanks, detective."

"Good luck, Doc."

Jax leaned in next to Doc and said warmly, "Nice to know you, Rick."

"Just make sure you don't portray me as a fool if this makes it into one of your shows, alright?"

"I promise," Jax replied with a genuine smile. "Maybe you could clue us in on your explanation of the deaths, so we can mention it before the credits roll?"

"I'll do my best."

They watched him drive away, then headed inside to recount the night's events to Beano and Bindi.

The following day, Jax was in the office early. Doc strolled in and surprised her. "Not like you to get in before midday, what's up?" she asked.

Doc sat at his desk, picked up a pen, and twiddled it between his fingers as he swivelled to face her, "Oh, I don't know, I couldn't sleep, been up all night … I can't figure out this case … you know me, if I don't have a logical handle on it, it becomes baggage that I don't want to lug around."

"Yeah it can take up too much brain space, I know. Tell you what, call Beano, meet him at Atomic studio play the conjuring and witness Choronzon's appearance first hand. But you'll need to do it before he gets there today and erases it," she proposed facetiously.

"No thanks, I'd rather have the baggage. As usual you're content with the supernatural explanation?"

"And are you happy to live with the unexplained flag?"

"Seems all of our cases have been non liquet from me."

"I wouldn't worry about it, Doc, someone has to hold the scientific view, and that person has always been you. Stranger that you write songs about the paranormal but believe otherwise."

"What songs?" he said disbelieving.

"Somewhere in my mind?"

"The lyric is to be interpreted by the individual … you see you hear it as supernatural, others would think it's just the working of the inner-self."

"Now that's bordering on transcendental."

Digger wandered in, "Who's going to the dentist?"

Both Jax and Doc looked at him with wrinkled brows and questioned simultaneously, "Uh?"

"You said dental, Jax," Digger said sitting behind his desk.

"No," Jax corrected, "I said transcendental, you only heard the end of the word."

"So it's a metaphysical debate is it? Don't tell me, Doc isn't convinced Choronzon existed while you Jax looked him in the eye and know it."

Jax smiled smugly, "Something like that."

"Well, I didn't meet Choronzon personally but I found his handiwork, so I'm afraid I have to side with you, Jax."

"And what makes anyone think it would be any other way ... brother and sister, you're as thick as thieves."

A phone rang Jax answered, "Hello, oh hi ... really! Where? I see. Anything we can do? Fine, okay, thanks." The expression on her face said it all as she reported, "That was Malone, the body of a jogger was found this morning in Bedlam Bay Garden ... her eyes were missing."

"That's right next to the old mental asylum where we were last night," Doc said.

"It could only have been Choronzon," Jax said, alarmed. "He couldn't have Sheila, so he went and found someone else."

The desk phone rang. Jax answered and was promptly summoned to a production meeting.

Jax entered Des Carter's office and sat beside Janet, both facing Carter behind his desk, who was twiddling a pen between his fingers.

"I just got off the phone with homicide. Seems you lot are in up to your necks in a murder investigation," Carter stated.

"Well, it's a lot more than a murder investigation; it's a Next File," Jax countered.

"No, it's not, Jax," Carter said emphatically.

Janet was shaking her head in support of Carter. "We can't report on a murder investigation, Jax, not until it's resolved by the police, the coroner, and the court."

"Three people have been horribly killed, Jax. That's a true crime case, not The Next Files. You need to find something more in keeping with the Next Files ethos as your next story. This one is a no-go."

Jax nodded understandingly, then said, "It's a shame. The story of a demon conjured by a backward occult incantation recorded by a death metal band sounds to me like a full-on Next File."

Carter and Janet seemed impressed. "You're right when you put it like that. Write it up and then shelve it until the case is over. It'll be perfect then," Carter said.

"Get the recording engineer, the band, and those girls to sign off on it so we don't lose it," Janet added.

Jax stood up. "I'll give you their details and leave that up to you guys; that's not our bag. Anything else?"

Carter shook his head. Once Jax had left the room, he told Janet, "She's learning fast."

"The three of them are brilliant. I don't know how they have the courage to do what they do," Janet responded.

Carter smiled and suggested, "Maybe it's just youthful naivety."

"That's exactly what makes the show work."

When Jax broke the news to Digger and Doc that the Hellhouse story was being shelved, their reaction was less dramatic than she had expected.

"Well, it's only to be expected, seeing it's an ongoing homicide," Doc commented casually.

"Or is it too intense for our audience?" Digger chimed in.

Jax leaned back in her chair behind the desk and clarified, "Janet thinks it doesn't exactly fit the Next Files paradigm, and I guess she's right—we're not a true crime show."

Digger snickered playfully, "Yeah, but everyone has their demons."

"Digger, we've all been trying to avoid that cliché," Jax laughed. "So, what's next for us, Digger? Got any new Next Files?"

"Well, there's a witness report of a UAP sighting from Hamilton Island up on the Barrier Reef," Digger suggested.

"Yeah, pull the other one," Jax snorted with a grin.

Doc got up and sat on the edge of his desk, arms crossed, "I don't know, sounds good to me."

Just then, the door swung open and Tilly breezed in, her cheer filling the room, "Hello, my lovelies, heard you've been out there chasing demons."

"We sure have," Jax responded.

"Must've been tough, everybody's got one," Tilly quipped, bursting into laughter. The other three just groaned. "Alright, alright, is it going to be like that today? Who's up for a coffee and a chocolate digestive?"

They all raised their hands.

"What about the fella down in Bega on the south coast, the Yowie Man? He reckons he's been tracking Yowies all over the country for years," Digger suggested, getting back onto the subject.

"Nah, we've got the bunyip story airing next week, we need something fresh," Doc pointed out.

"True," Jax agreed.

"What about the mermaid that was caught in a fisherman's net in Borneo?" Digger threw out.

That idea fired Jax up; she sat up straight, eager, "I like that, when was that?"

"I dunno, I just made it up," Digger confessed with a cackle.

"Digger!" Jax scolded. Tilly returned with three mugs of coffee and a plate of biscuits. Digger and Doc dived into the biscuits.

"Hey, leave one for your boss," Tilly teased.

Digger reluctantly put a biscuit back on the plate. Jax shot him a raised eyebrow, prompting him to sheepishly return another.

As Tilly was leaving, she paused in the doorway, throwing out casually, "Oh, the news on tele this morning mentioned a dinosaur sighting on a volcanic island in Papua New Guinea."

"Now you're talking," Digger said, his eyes lighting up. Tilly offered them a big, knowing grin and left as the three of them eagerly jumped onto their computers to research the report.

Don't miss the next monsterous Next File:

# DINOSAUR